Cameron Rhyder's Legs
MATTHEW KRESSEL

Five thousand young men and women crowd this music hall tonight, and one of them is the soul I must erase from existence. How many she has killed I cannot say. To suggest a number is a sin. How can we count those who no longer exist? I once had a family, a husband, eight children. A life and a future. But all this has been timelost, expunged from history. And so I will expunge her. Except I've no idea who she is. Or *he*, for that matter. In this Now, gender and dress make a difference.

Today, I'm female. My boxy eyeglasses, fashionably retro, hide a rainbow of sensors. I scan their eyes for tells, hunt their mind-detritus for fear. It's hard to see who's just stoned and who's got something to hide. My gold digital watch, also retro, holo-def hicodes what my eyes miss.

I wear tight black jeans and a persistent smirk as if I'm entitled to things I don't deserve. My body is average, my skin tawny-light, my black hair medium-length, nose unremarkable. I'm a mayfly, engineered to be forgotten. I scan their bodies for changes since their last instance in this Now as they glimpse, then immediately forget me.

They're here for the Goo Globbers, the glammed-out rock quartet that howls like a synaptic re-write. The crowd applauds far too much at the end of the first song, which I gauge as a covert attempt to escape their unexpressed fears. Unlike me, they cannot know their future.

The singer Scott Mohl croons, "*The day ends with the setting sun, the flower wilts, its colors run,*" and the crowd swoons in a haze of marijuana smoke and purple spotlights. But the colored patterns flicker-flash too precisely to be Now-native. Someone's using lustre-tech to coerce brain states, but this tech won't exist for another fifty years.

Scott Mohl's honied voice reverberates under my feet as I weave through dancing bodies, scanning, scanning. Their dilated eyes make my probes of their forebrains a cakewalk.

I scan a young, fire-haired woman with leafy green eyes. Cat's-eye glasses on the end of her nose twinkle with rhinestones. Her lips part as my retinal shines a maser deep into her pupils at frequencies attuned to her neurons, hijacking her brain and dumping her memories into mine.

She has been in this Now before, my Archives tell me, in nine hundred and eighty one instances. I scan her blackbody signature for aberrations.

I find one, of course. When she was seven, a pebble got caught in her bicycle wheel, and she crashed and broke her leg. And because she couldn't go outside, she hung around the house and listened to her brother's music collection, which spawned an interest in the musical subgenre of alternative retro-punk-fuzz-fusion, which led her, eighteen years, five months and four days later to this Goo Globbers concert. She's kept the pebble with her all this time, a totem to the gods of fate. Her hand fiddles with it in her pocket just now.

And it was We, The Hands of Brahma, who placed the pebble two millimeters to the left from where it was the last time. And because of our Correction, her recovery lasted two days, seven hours longer, and her interest in retro-punk-fuzz-fusion solidified, and in this Now she arrived to this concert six minutes and nine seconds earlier. She took her place beside the bar, drinking her rum sours every nineteen minutes forty-one seconds, on average, as she always does. Her early arrival forced a tall male of South-Asian genetics to move one meter to the left and scratch his nose, which he has never done in any Nows before.

I log this through Twitter, spread across hundreds of accounts, in a series of steganographically-encoded photographs I take with my camera-phone. My Tweets will find their way to the future via the Library of Congress Twitter Archive, where my superiors will read and dissect them nine hundred years hence.

I flash the woman's short-term memory and set her free two seconds after we've met eyes. I'm careful not to leave memories. To do so would risk not only my life but the Great Mission itself. Her cat's-eye glasses sparkle as she moves on.

There may be hundreds of Anachronists hiding in the crowd. If they find me they'll erase me from existence, or worse, rewrite my memories so I'll fight and die for their sick cause.

We'll do the same to them, of course. War is war, after all. But any timelost fool can see that what we're doing is nothing short of saving the Cosmos from chaos, their ultimate goal.

Scott Mohl belts, "*The shadows of our yesterdays fall across my face, who are we but dust and loam, adrift in inner space?*" The audience sways blissfully as the stage lights let loose a spray of brain-calming

CLARKESWORLD

NOVEMBER 2014 · ISSUE 98

FICTION

NON-FICTION

Neil Clarke: Publisher/Editor-in-Chief
Sean Wallace: Editor
Kate Baker: Non-Fiction Editor/Podcast Director
Gardner Dozois: Reprint Editor

Clarkesworld Magazine (ISSN: 1937-7843) • Issue 98 • November 2014

© Clarkesworld Magazine, 2014
www.clarkesworldmagazine.com

frequencies. Someone wants this crowd wide open and suggestible. Us, or them?

I scan and record Corrections by the thousand-fold. The dancing acne-faced kid with too much energy (a passing word from a stranger began the causal chain that led him here). The pink-haired girl typing into her phone and taking pictures of herself (a book left open to a particular passage). The brawny security guard with crossed arms and a dour expression (a can of soup, moved from one shelf to another). Even Scott Mohl, hopping around stage in his glittery cape and leather pants (a whiff of sunscreen on a winter's day). All have been Corrected thousands of times. People native to this Now believe they live such insignificant lives. If only they knew their grand purpose, how we gently nudge them toward enlightenment one millimeter at a time.

For We, the Hands of Brahma, have sent countless operatives here, via circuitous and parallel Nows, though those histories, if I have ever known them, have been erased from my memory. (To break the Causal Chain is a sin; the True Time must be preserved.) Just the same, the Anachronists have sent myriad operatives here. Nearly a million times they have nudged, forced, and heaved this moment away from the True Time. And always, we push it back. It's been a cat and mouse game for eons. In short, I'm not alone.

Ninety-quintillion qubit hours of b-tree analysis and billions of timelost souls point to an event *here* as Ultimate Cause. Something happens tonight—specifically what, we have not yet determined—which through a complex series of causally chained events, will bring about the end of the Varaha Kalpa, Brahma's Day. Time as we know it will cease. Atoms will fly apart. Cause and effect will lose meaning.

The Cosmos will die.

And oh, how I long for that moment with all my heart! For in that moment the Living Cosmos will be reborn. The timelost will be found. Death will end. Blessed is her name, Tat Tvam Asi, That Thou Art, who dies so that we may live! If I find and erase my target tonight, all this glory shall come to pass.

"I'm told we have a guest here tonight," Scott Mohl says to whoops and jeers from the crowd. "The lovely Cameron Rhyder." He holds out a hand toward the VIP dais at stage right. "Hey, doll," he says, "join us?"

The crowd turns to the disgraced former actress and one-time lover of Scott Mohl, Cameron Rhyder, sitting on the VIP dais. She leans forward in her seat and takes a sip of scotch, while on the dancefloor beside her, an olive-skinned man with a Van Dyke beard stares at her legs.

This is wrong. In four thousand previous Nows his gaze has never lingered on her legs for so long. As Ms. Cameron Rhyder slowly rises from her seat, I shove through the crowd and yank out my timeclaw.

The Brahma Brute smirks over me as she plucks a hair from my Van Dyke beard and puts it in a glass phial. She's had me down deep, scoured my brain for secrets, and I'm all fogged up.

She adjusts her boxy eyeglasses, 21st-century retro, that hide an array of sensors and weaponry. Her gold watch not only tells time but helps her manipulate it.

These Brutes brainwashed Myra, my wife. She died in the Battle of Pendulum, fighting for them. I had to explain to Jacob, our son, why she sent us all those hateful messages, why she cursed our family to her last breath. And when Jacob asked me if he would one day hate me too, I knew I had to join the fight to save us all.

I lay strapped to the Brute's chair in this dark, humid cave, where crude paintings of violent hunts and antlered gods on the walls tell a story that might have happened last week.

"This will hurt worse than anything you can imagine, 219," the Brute says. These freaks switch bodies so often they don't even use names.

My Goo Globbers t-shirt reeks of marijuana from the music hall. My temple throbs where she hooked me with her timeclaw and yanked me backward through time.

Ten blank-eyed Variants stand by the cave exit, their crisp white uniforms bright against the stone walls. The electric blue numbers on their breasts glow like a frozen stopwatch.

"I'll take whatever you got," I say.

My thoughts stutter as hot red beams shine onto me from hanging panels. They yank out data written into my junk DNA by the petabyte: the number of times my genes have be rewritten (forty seven), my taste for sour sweets (borderline addictive), my fetish for women in yellow sports socks (admittedly weird).

"You have a pocket of gas in your large intestine," she says. "Twenty-first century polysaturated fats do not suit you."

"I could fart, if you want."

"You've turned off input from your sympathetic nervous system. But I can bypass your physical body and send thoughts directly into your mind."

Suddenly I can't breathe: I'm being hung from a tree! The pain is obscene, but I've trained for this.

She stops the pain, and I try to gasp with dignity but fail.

"That was nothing," she says. "I can simulate being eaten alive by rats, falling from a great height onto stone, freezing to death in icy water, and other such horrors. But I've no desire to be cruel."

I silently repeat my trigger phrase, and the post-hypnotic suggestion calms my fear. But my calm is fraught. Jacob will grow up without parents, without someone to lead him through the dark. "I won't let you destroy the universe," I say.

She sighs. "Is that the best you have, 219? I expected more from an Anachronist. I can rewrite your memories, make you docile and obedient, like my Variants here." She gestures to the blank-eyed souls surrounding us. I recognize two from my time at Buenos Aires bootcamp.

Davey Blackwood had a wife and three daughters. Sandra Chatterjee was finishing her Ph.D. in Temporal Dynamics when she got drafted. Now they'd kill their own child if this Brute ordered them to.

I try to muster confidence. "Do what you must."

A duplicate Variant 175—another Sandra Chatterjee—enters the cave. She appears in all ways identical to the Variant 175 standing by the cave mouth. The two meet eyes, exchange data. "I come from an instance seven minutes and forty-two seconds ahead of this Now," the second says. "Madam Interrogator 991, please note that a forced neural rewrite will destroy any possible recovery of information from this patient. Your future self respectfully requests you try another method."

The original Variant 175 waits until the duplicate has finished, then she heads for the cave exit to activate her timeclaw and close the loop.

"You see how hopeless it is, 219?" the Brute says. "Our Variant will leap back in time at exactly seven minutes and forty-two seconds from the moment her future self arrived and she will repeat those words to me exactly as she has heard them, thus preserving the True Time. Though the original cause of the message is timelost, we have gained information from the Void. Such are the wonders of the great Tat Tvam Asi, blessed is Her Glorious Name, who Herself exists Without Cause!"

"Your sick philosophy has murdered trillions."

Variant 293 runs into the cave and says, "I come from an instance two minutes and nine seconds ahead of this Now. Stop! Patient 219's neural DNA is booby trapped with singularity bombs. In my instance, Variant 9641 emerged from the timestream charred and burnt from an explosion, which she said destroyed a significant portion of North America. She died immediately. Your future self kindly requests you do not scrub his neural DNA." The original Variant 293 leaves the cave.

"Again!" she says, "True Time is preserved, blessed is The Causeless One!" She smiles at me, her pupils like swirling black holes in the bright lights. "Do you understand yet?" she says. "Anything you do, we predict. We have Variants spread throughout history, ready to timeleap at a moment's notice." She smiles seductively. "Now, are you ready to talk?"

"There's nothing to say."

"I beg to differ." I feel as if I'm being torn apart by wolves, stoned to death by an angry mob, hung upside down in a frigid river by my testicles. But this is just pain, and pain will fade. *All* will fade soon enough.

"Now, what was your assignment in the music hall? Why did your eyes linger on Cameron Rhyder's legs three point seven seconds longer than any previous instance?"

I take several breaths to compose myself. "You will fail this interrogation, as you have always failed, and you know it. A Variant would have arrived by now with all the information, extracted from a future Now. That is how it works, isn't it?"

"No," she says. "Because that information hasn't arrived, the only answer is that *this* is the Now in which I extract information from you and which I later choose not to send back in time for reasons unknown to me now."

"You know that's not true. As soon as you find out what I know, you'll scatter the knowledge through time. But that has not happened because my task is already done. I've completed my assignment. We've already won."

"If the Anachronists have won, as you say, then why are you bound in a cave, on the same spot where the Goo Globbers will take the stage ten thousand years from today, and why are we still at war? In short, why do we exist? You *cannot* have won."

"We are here because this is how it happens."

"*What* happens, 219?"

She pushes my brain into an alpha state and ramps up my oxytocin sensitivity. Now when I look into her eyes I see a caring mother, only concerned with imparting love and securing my everlasting well-being. I've been trained to resist these coercions too. "What do you think will happen when Brahma's Day ends?" I ask.

Her eyes brighten. "With the close of the Varaha Kalpa, all will become One Glorious Unity. We will merge with the Blessed Tat Tvam Asi. There will be no more time, no more duality, no more separation of object and observer. We will become God." The Variants by the door smile.

"That's a delusion. The end of Brahma's Day will destroy everything. Nothing but chaos will remain. Energy will be unable to coalesce into matter because time no longer exists. You speak of a Golden Age, but of what, when, and where will this Golden Age exist?"

"What, when and where are meaningless terms when speaking of the Blessed Tat Tvam Asi who has no substance, duration, nor place."

"But *we* are human beings who exist in space and time, with breadth and duration. Destroy that and you destroy us. All the galaxies and countless stars. All the worlds teeming with life. You destroy *everything* that has ever been."

"Not destroy, 219. *Revert.* The Cosmos will return to its primordial unity."

"You want to reverse billions of years of evolution for the sake of a delusion."

"We want to take evolution to the next step."

"You want to extinguish all life."

"You motives are transparent, 219. You attack my core beliefs in an attempt to find weaknesses to exploit."

I try to shake my head, but the straps don't allow it. "No, I'm pointing out that our continued existence proves that you're wrong, that we've already won and you've already lost. If time has no meaning to your Timeless God, then the close of Brahma's Day has already occurred in some Now. If you have succeeded, then this Now could not possibly continue to exist."

"You lack understanding of our theology, 219. Because we exist, it is *this* Now where we succeed in closing Brahma's Day. We believe we all live in the True Time, the fixed Now that will bring about the close of the Varaha Kalpa. The True Time, like the stem of a lotus flower, is long and seemingly endless. But at its eventual end the Glorious Unity of Brahma blossoms. If we exist, then we must be living in True Time, the last and ultimate reality that leads to the Godhead."

"Wrong again," I say. Jacob floats before my closed eyelids, his hands grasping for me in the dark. "Because this moment will soon be timelost."

"There is no way you can be conscious of your own nonexistence."

"Oh, yes I can."

"And how is that, 219?"

I swallow. What choice do I have? "Because no one has come to warn you this time. Oh, Jacob, forgive me." Then I trigger the singularity bomb hidden in my brain stem.

I scratch my three days of scruff and light a menthol cigarette as I stand beside the bar after the opening act ends. People rush to the bathrooms in droves before the Goo Globbers will take the stage. The air grows thick with smoke and the stank of beer. It's too hot for my leather jacket, my boots make my feet blister, and my balls sweat.

I hate pretending to be someone I'm not. Once, my Archives tell me, I composed Neo-Baroque symphonies at a conservatory that won't be built for another four hundred years. I was world renown and in love with a young man from Nigeria. But this past has been timelost. The Anachronists washed away my joy into the sea of Has Never Been. I don't remember his name or his face, but I know that when the Varaha Kalpa ends, I'll embrace my lover again. We will all reunite with the timelost, and together we will write symphonies with the Godhead herself.

My phone vibrates in my pocket. Someone has tagged a picture on Instagram with my handle: it's the line to the bathroom that I'm looking at now, except the queue has moved forward a few paces. The encoded data says the photo is from the future and that I took it. On the graffitied wall is a faded sentence written in Eurogeek, a language that won't exist for two hundred years, but the words are spelled phonetically in ancient Akkadian. It's overlaid with newer graffiti and dozens of band stickers and is at least ten years old in this Now. The words read, "The woman directly underneath these words is Agent 991 of the Hands of Brahma. Make contact with her and share all information. Blessed be Tat Tvam Asi."

The queue moves so that it matches the photo exactly. Right under the Akkadian letters is a woman with black hair, boxy retro eyeglasses, a gold digital watch, tight jeans. I lift my phone, take a picture of the queue at the precise moment, and email it to a server in Togo, where through the blessing of the Timeless One it will find its way to the future. The Causal Chain must be preserved.

I approach the woman and hold out an unlit cigarette. "Got a light?"

"Don't smoke," she says.

I flash my retinal maser into her eyes, and there's a brief moment where we pass encryption keys, entangled photons, and subatomic handshakes to negotiate deeper levels of trust. She's one of us, but I outrank her, thank the Godhead.

I'm Agent 337, I transmit through the maser. *I've been authorized to divulge all.*

WHY ARE YOU BREAKING COM SILENCE? she transmits.

Because I've found him.

Him? Even through the maser I sense her disbelief.

The last Anachronist to stand in our way before the Glorious Unity. He's beside the stage, next to the VIP section. He's wearing a Goo Globbers t-shirt, has ruffled brown hair, brown-olive skin, and a Van Dyke beard. I transmit his DNA marker and black body signature to her.

Why come to me? she says. *You could erase him yourself.* She scans the people nearby. *This dialog risks outing us. Making contact is not in my mission profile.*

In my last instance in this Now, I say, *a taxi killed me as I crossed the street outside this concert hall. The Anachronists are never so overt. They know that I know his identity, and they're desperate. You see why I cannot erase him myself?*

It could have been a true accident, she says.

True? I hope you know better, 991. But, you're right, there's more. In your last instantiation of this Now you brought the suspect backtime to the year 10,981 BCE. You interrogated him, but were killed when he detonated a singularity bomb embedded in his lower brain stem. We let him destroy you so that the Anachronists would believe they have the upper hand.

This isn't strange, she says. *I've been killed hundreds of times. Without concrete evidence, how can I proceed?*

It's an order.

And if we erase the wrong person based on your whim, eons of labor will be lost. We might end up infinitely farther from the close of Brahma's Day. I'm sorry, but without confirmation, I cannot proceed. She lifts her phone, about to transmit a record of our conversation through Instagram.

I've no time for this. I outrank her and have privileges over her retinal. I flash her short-term memory and write my orders onto her prefrontal cortex. I write twice, just to be sure.

Got it, yes, sir, she says, lowering her phone. *Suspect at stage right, male, twenty-six, olive-skin, Van Dyke beard, Goo Globbers t-shirt. Pursue and erase.*

I purge her memories of our encounter, and our conversation ends two point five seconds after it began. Outwardly she shows no signs of change. She's one of them now, a civilian. She will follow my instructions without knowing it. "Maybe I will take that cigarette," she says. I light it and she takes a drag, then thanks me before she saunters toward the stage.

It's my turn to go and I enter a stall that reeks of weed and piss. As I close the latch I can't stop smiling. Our greatest moment so close at hand! Brahma's Day will end! The timelost will be found! Blessed is her name, Tat Tvam Asi, That Thou Art, who dies so that we may live!

A fire-haired woman pushes into the stall, and the rhinestones on her cat's-eye glasses twinkle like fairy dust. Her leafy-green eyes hold me a bit too long before I realize I've been hijacked.

"Goodnight, honey," she says, pressing her lips against mine.

No! Wait? What was I just thinking? What was I just doing?

She stares at me, this beautiful, beautiful creature. I'd do anything for her. I'd die for her.

"Change of plans," she says as she presses something tiny and hard into my palm. "A little gift for Ms. Cameron Rhyder."

Cameron Rhyder is a stupid name, but I wear it proudly.

The suit greets me as I enter the backstage doors. "Ms. Rhyder, I'll take you to your seat." He doesn't know he escorts the world's last hope, the culmination of eons of labor. His smile is forced, perfunctory. I remember making it when I was in his body.

Roadies wake from their stupor as I pass forests of lights and gear. Red cups pop like fruit from labyrinths of black boxes. Their cigarette smoke curls into vortices as I walk past them. It takes them a second.

Holy fuck, that's Cameron Rhyder, that chick from that movie, what's it called? The Doggerel Star with Jimmy Everwood and Kristina Goodman.

Shit, what happened to her?

I know their thoughts from other Nows, when I inhabited their bodies: how I got old but am still fuckable, how my career tanked after I got busted in the back of an RV parked beside that Brooklyn fish-packing warehouse while sniffing crushed oxy from a nineteen year old's penis with forty thousand dollars of stolen coke hidden in the trunk. The coke wasn't mine. The douchebag with the big cock stole it from his friend, who ratted him out so he wouldn't get wacked by the mob. But try explaining that to a public who hates celebrities only slightly more than they adore them. They threw me to the wolves, then the wolves threw me to the scavengers.

I suppose all of this would've mattered to the real Cameron Rhyder. That entity sleeps way down in the substrata of this body's brain. I feel her try to wake every few minutes, as she has for the past two days I've been inside her mind. I nudge her back to sleep with sweet memories of douchebag inside of her.

The suited man smacks open the steel door, and the sounds of the audience explode in my ears. He throws aside a curtain to reveal a thousand wiggling faces, barely conscious worms tenaciously clinging to life. They've no idea they eat death, that they suffice on rot.

They call it nihilism. I call it genocide.

The suit leads me to a table third from the stage. The crimson-dressed two-tops rest on a VIP dais a meter above the dance floor, like a king's court. But we're not the highlight. That's the stage, where all kings will abdicate their thrones tonight, where all subjects will shed

10

their chains. I take my seat, order a single malt from a pimple-faced kid who notices then pretends not to recognize me.

Others do. People whisper and point and avert their eyes. They've seen me on a screen, a whole dimension flattened, and yet I've become larger in their eyes. But in person, in all three dimensions, I'm lessened, made human. That's why they stare, because in seeing me lowered to a mere person they raise themselves up.

I'm fine with that. Equal footing is what I'm after.

The lights dim and the crowd roars, raucous to the point of dangerous. They're ready to pop. The bouncers straighten, check their earbuds. Under cover of the noise, shadows sneak onto the stage and take their positions. The roar grows.

White spotlights flash onto the lead singer. The silver cape over his shoulders reflects a sky of constellations up the walls. Orion, Cassiopeia, Canis Major. Their positions match the sky outside just now. He slams a power chord and the cheers fade under the heavy crunch of distortion.

As the chord hangs he sings, "*Where has my innocence run? Where is my peaceful weather? How sunny were the days, when days . . . they ran forever.*"

The lights go up and it's spectral chaos. The band joins in with a dominant seventh. It is fierce, the three-seven time, the swooning melody.

Damn. Even after all these eons, after so much death and horror, their music still moves me. That's why it had to be them, the Goo Globbers, the only band in Eternity who can thwart oblivion.

I send a command to the stage lights, to the lustre-tech I embedded four years ago. They switch on full spectrum, and everyone's mind is pried wide open, modulated by the lights and a thousand other methods. But I set the other manipulators in previous Nows; there's no way to know for sure if all but the lustre remains unadultered.

The crowd writhes on the dancefloor beneath us. One young man with a Van Dyke beard, olive skin, and a Goo Globbers t-shirt points at me, his fingers only inches from my ankles. "Dude," he shouts to his friend, "that's Cameron Rhyder's legs!"

His friend shakes his head, embarrassed.

I ignore them and sip my scotch exactly as I have done four thousand six hundred and eighty times before.

A cute guy two tables over smiles and gives me a sympathetic expression. When I was in his body in a previous Now I learned he's got undiagnosed cancer of the prostate. He'll be dead in eighteen months. The real Cameron Rhyder would probably have fucked him in a shitty hotel room nearby, crying afterward over how far she's fallen from her glory days. My body warms instinctively at the thought of his body pressing into mine.

The song ends, bleeds into another. A bluesy, jazzing jam, lots of fuzz. The drummer sweats rivers.

A smirking woman with dark hair, boxy eyeglasses, tight jeans, and a gold digital watch sidles up to the dancing men beside me. They gawk and stare at her body.

Everyone's mind is wide open. Impulses are laid bare. Privacy is a discarded piece of clothing.

She dances before the men, rubbing against them as the beat progresses. She's flushed, shivering, overheated, her eyes rolled back into her head, all signs she's orgasmic. It's a side effect of the lustre. I count seventy-one men and women currently experiencing orgasm.

Do they know to whom they sacrifice their lust, to what wiggling chaos of unborn nightmare they pray? They writhe mindlessly, their imagination dead. They dream others' dreams and think them their own. Nihilism has been chosen for them because they haven't learned how to choose for themselves.

Until tonight. Until me. I will get this right this time. I must.

The bespectacled girl moves behind the Van Dyke. She plays his chest like a guitar, brushes her hand over his crotch.

Three bodies back, a man in a leather jacket and two days of scruff lights a cigarette and considers me coolly, as he always does. A roadie sneaks out from a curtain onto the VIP dais. He squats beside me and says, "Scott—" that is, Scott Mohl, lead singer of the Goo Globbers, "—heard you're here. Would you do a duet?"

Ms. Rhyder had a brief post-acting career as a singer-songwriter. Until the drug bust. "What song?"

His breath reeks of cigarettes. "Autumn Days?"

From their first album. "Too dreary. How about My Disposition?" It's a poem I, in Cameron's body, wrote when I left Scott for good one morning a thousand Nows ago. He recorded it under his name as a kind of revenge, turned it into a hit. And if we sing it tonight, we'll be singing *my* words to the most important audience in history.

"I'll ask," the roadie says.

"When?"

"I'll signal you."

I nod, feign flattery and nerves as he walks back into the shadows. The latches have been set, the trap is ready.

The song ends. Scott makes obeisances to the crowd, sips from a water bottle. "How y'all doing tonight?"

Cheers erupt. Some awaken from trances to shock and fear at their loss of control. Six people are freaking out. Nine more quiver from orgasm.

The roadie whispers to the bassist, who says something off-mic to Scott.

"I'm told we have a guest here tonight."

Whoops and jeers. Everyone knows of our little tryst.

"The lovely Cameron Rhyder." Lunchroom boos, cheers. The roadie's waving at me. "Hey, doll," says Scott, his hand outstretched toward me, "join us?"

I stand to whistles and cheers. "Got any blow?" one screams. Another: "Cameron, we love you!"

A spotlight, hot and blinding, swivels onto me as I step on stage. I can't see, but just as well. "Hiya, Cammy," Scott says off mic, then he gives me a hug. In private, he'd be just as likely to tell me off.

"Ninth Division?" he says.

This is wrong. "How about My Disposition?"

"I'm tired of it." Then to the band, "Ninth Division, on four. One . . . two . . . three . . . "

And just like that we're performing the wrong song. I fucked up, somewhere. Now I have to play along, to sing his thinly veiled polemic on the evils of the military industrial complex, told as a clichéd love story between two star-crossed lovers.

Scott knows I hate this song, but not for the reasons he thinks. Its angry baseline becomes the thing it criticizes: unchecked rage. Played for a crowd this open, it will solidify the destructive mentality. It promises freedom, but makes them slaves.

I can't allow this. I've worked too hard, too long to get here. I activate the nano I've placed in the bassist's brain and ramp up his sensitivity to THC. The joint he smoked an hour ago and thought he was coming down from now gets fifty times stronger.

His timing skews. He misses notes.

Scott and I sing, "*I can't see above the wall, but I know you're on the other side,*" as the audience cringes at the bassist's errors. They're being programmed for sure, but it won't be as deep.

We give the song a respectful end, bow, and the audience responds with a weak applause. We're losing them.

"What the fuck, man?" the drummer shouts to the bassist.

"I'm good," the bassist says, looking green.

I use the lull and jump in. "My Disposition on four, ready? One . . . two . . . three . . . "

The drummer pounds the kettles as Scott cocks his head at me and smiles wryly. He knows he's been beaten. I drop the bassist's high and ramp up the band's dopamine. I need them at their best.

And they're so fucking together it's magical. We've yanked the audience back from the abyss. I sing, "*All of us, every one, have been the other, you know, at one time or another.*"

And Scott replies, "*And the other, mother, sister, lover, would you know them by their cover?*"

On the dance floor below my table the dark-haired girl in the boxy glasses and gold watch spins around and tongue-kisses the man with the Van Dyke. I ramp up the lustre-tech to max, flood the air with massive doses of oxytocin, coerce the frequencies of my voice to resonate blissfully with human sensory meridians. Their bodies in ecstasy, they're open to anything.

I step forward and belt, "*I have been you and you have been me, all throughout Eternity. Don't you get it? Don't you see? You have been that one and that one is me.*"

The guitarist riffs through the interlude, making amateurs of the greats. The drummer is picking out rhythms he didn't know existed. The bassist is plucking chords in heroic timing. Scott's voice is hitting notes birds can't reach.

And when I sing the next verse they will awaken to the stark truth. We've been fighting this war for so long, in so many variations that in this Now, in this moment, I, the entity that stands in Cameron Rhyder's body, have been every one of them. I, who no longer have a name, remember them all.

I have been the smirking bouncer, and I have been the bemused roadies. And I was Scott Mohl and every member of the Goo Globbers. And was the man who will die of cancer, and I have been both halves of the couple kissing beneath my seat.

Inside their fragile bodies I have traveled forward and backward through time. With their hands I have slaughtered and erased and destroyed. I have had my mind rewritten and reprogrammed more than a billion times. The words I sing to them are utterly true: *I have been you and you have been me, all throughout Eternity.*

And when I sing my next verse, they will awaken to this truth. The Anachronists will see the futility of their cause. The Hands of Brahma will know that the Unity they seek is already here, in my body, this flesh of Cameron Rhyder. They have already become One. Brahma's Day ends with me.

And here I go, second stanza, moment of truth.

I step forward, but something sharp jabs my left foot. There's something in my shoe. The pain makes me stumble, and my heel catches a wire. I'm thrown forward, down and hard, over the edge of the stage.

My head slams into the floor. My neck cracks. The pain is obscene, so I switch it off.

Screams, not my own. I can't move! My heart rate spikes. My neck is broken. I'll be dead in seconds!

No! All of this mustn't be for nothing! I was so close to showing them the truth: when we kill each other, we kill ourselves. Don't you all see? We're maggots feasting on our own body!

I was going to wake them up. I was going to inject this knowledge into them, so that for one instant we'd become a singular mind, one conscious entity, who could stop this madness forever.

Blackness pours into my vision as people surround me. The scruffy man in the leather jacket photographs me with his camera phone. The young woman with cat's-eye glasses and leafy green eyes leans over and checks my pulse. She reaches for my shoe, which has fallen off, and pulls out something tiny from the heel. A pebble. The same pebble that threw her/me/us off our bicycle so many years ago. She puts it in her pocket and smiles at me.

Her pupils dilate rapidly, a sign of a hijack letting go. Whoever was in her has fled. She's confused, frozen. Suggestible. Here's my last chance.

I activate my maser and write deep into her mind. I've only got seconds before death. On the way home, shaken and sickened by what she's seen, she'll hum "My Disposition" without realizing it. The words will be stuck in her head for months. She'll never be able to think of the song the same way again.

For Arthur C.

ABOUT THE AUTHOR

Matthew Kressel's work has appeared in *Lightspeed, Clarkesworld, io9.com, Beneath Ceaseless Skies, Interzone, Electric Velocipede, Apex Magazine,* and the anthologies *Naked City, After, The People of the Book,* and other markets. His story "The Sounds of Old Earth" was recently nominated for a Nebula Award. He has been nominated for a World Fantasy Award for his work editing *Sybil's Garage,* a speculative fiction 'zine he published from 2003-2010. Currently he co-hosts the Fantastic Fiction at KGB reading series in Manhattan with Ellen Datlow. He is a member of the Altered Fluid writers group, and in his spare time he studies the Yiddish language.

Pernicious Romance
ROBERT REED

There are no suspects.

We know the vehicle was serviced by the school motor pool, but there were numerous locations and intervals where clever hands could have added a malicious device. Subsequent investigations have exonerated university employees as well as the student programmer responsible for the custom software piloting the giant football helmet. Investigations continue, but authorities no longer issue reports, claiming undiminished interest even as the work thins to fewer agencies and skeletal crews.

Even in retrospect, nothing about the football game appears out of the ordinary. Fiercely contested and low scoring, the battle matched every expectation up until halftime. Then the marching band played three numbers—a solid performance, perhaps even inspired. Once the band relinquished the field, the stadium lights were set low, and that was when the giant football helmet, lit up with the school colors, sprinted across the darkened turf, deploying an LED hose in its wake. The tradition was three years old. The competitive game and mild October weather insured that the stands were nearly full. With a flowing, artistic script, the home team's name was being written with the hose. Onlookers assumed a simple malfunction when the helmet stopped on the fifty-yard line. Perhaps seven seconds passed. Unfortunately there is no video recording of the event. A significant EMP event came with the attack, destroying the data from security cameras as well as amateur videos. The entire campus and half of the city were plunged into a prolonged blackout. But using the scorched rubber turf as a marker, it appears that the device, whatever its nature, was set near the back of the helmet, and its detonation consumed both the helmet and golf cart, leaving behind dust but almost no shrapnel.

As a rule, the first victims to "recover" were located in the most distant portions of the stadium. People high above the south end zone were two hundred and twenty yards from the device, give or take. Most would have been watching the darkened field and the progress of their school's helmet. Many would have been yelling out letters. Witnesses willing to discuss the event claim one of two scenarios: A bolt of light fell from the cloudless, moonless sky. "Lightning" is the most common word. "A laser beam" is also popular. But there are other accounts, equally certain, describing a flame or beam leaping up from the ground, presumably when the cart and helmet were vaporized.

Regardless of perpetrators, the attack was immediately blamed on terrorists.

That opinion hardened too quickly and too deeply, we believe.

These were enormous energies on display. There is no question about that. Which leaves us to wonder how any terrorist group could have mastered what appears to be a new technology—a set of tools that nobody else understands.

Cold as it sounds, we should feel thankful. In the end, only fifty-eight people were killed directly by the blast, while another thirty-nine succumbed to falls and head wounds. If casualties were the goal, these high-tech murderers could have ignited their weapon late in the first half, while the helmet was parked on the crowded sidelines. Unless of course the device was a demonstration event or a spectacular dud. Numerous public voices have made those bold claims, ignoring the absence of evidence. What is known is that nearly seventy thousand people were inside the stadium. Every survivor lost consciousness, some remaining that way until this day. And as a direct result, our country hasn't seen a major sporting event for sixteen months, and it is the same across most of the world. Nobody wants to risk a repeat of that terrible Saturday night.

Except for a large portion of the victims, that is.

Case Study:

Today MK is a thirty-one-year-old woman, single and employed. As an undergraduate, she played in the school band, and that's why the halftime show was her primary focus. But her little brother waited too long to purchase tickets, and that's why they had the worst possible seats, and that's why they were standing high up in the southern end of stadium, two hundred and twenty-three yards from the blast site.

MK remembers the band's three songs and then the helmet writing PANTHERS across the unlit field. The vehicle stopped while it was crossing the T, which wasn't right, and she immediately turned to her brother. She recalls laughing, telling him that this sort of shit wouldn't have happened when Dr. Kalin was in charge of the band.

MK had played the snare drums, as did her brother after her.

Her brother turned toward her, presumably to respond.

Both saw a brilliant flash of golden light.

Yes, she was sure. The light was definitely gold.

Panther Stadium is a bowl of concrete and steel with oak boards for seats and numerous steel railings. The stadium is quite steep near the top. Several people close to MK fractured their skulls when they collapsed. But in general, surprisingly few of the victims were injured. Evidence shows that the lowest rows felt the effects first, and like a wave dispersing across water, the people above collapsed in a very orderly fashion, falling on the bodies before them.

Intentional or not, that was another factor in the paucity of deaths.

People outside the stadium, including a small portion of the campus police and ambulance attendants, suffered moments of vertigo but never lost consciousness. After perhaps thirty seconds of confusion, those few hundred people entered to discover thousands of motionless, apparently helpless bodies. Yet these victims weren't unconscious, not in any normal sense. Every living person was breathing quickly and deeply, as if doing considerable labor. Some of those early responders reported a smell like perfume. But not everyone. The scope of the disaster and the total blackout led to panic, even among those with emergency training. But one campus police officer, armed with a working flashlight, climbed to the top row of the southern end of the stadium, and that's why she was first to come across a victim who was regaining consciousness.

MK has that distinction.

The officer knelt over the young woman. MK remembers her rescuer. In fact, she has talked at length about the pain and terror in that stranger's face.

"Are you okay?" the officer asked.

"Yeah," MK said.

In fact, she felt perfectly fine.

The officer held up a hand.

"Three fingers," MK answered, before the question was asked.

Then she sat up on her own power, lightheaded but not disabled. There were thousands of bodies below, not one of them moving. Yet she heard a peculiar sound, diffuse and gray and not quiet, and after a moment she realized how hard everybody was breathing.

"Something's happened," she said calmly.

"A bomb went off," the officer said. "You were knocked unconscious."

"No," MK said.

"Yes," the officer told her. She was still holding up the three fingers, and the hand was trembling. "Every last one you . . . knocked out."

MK said, "No."

"You were," the officer insisted.

"For how long?" MK asked.

The officer tried to make that calculation. But her cellphone was dead, and fear had distorted her sense of time.

"It's been a week," MK guessed.

"A week? Since you fell over?"

"Yes."

"No. It's been fifteen minutes, tops."

MK's brother, BK, was unconscious like the others, and then his breathing slowed. With a sigh, he opened his eyes. His forehead was scraped, but otherwise, he was unharmed and remarkably alert, sitting up beside his sister.

MK touched his wound.

"I didn't see you," she said.

BK agreed. "I didn't see you either."

The officer watched the conversation.

"This cop says fifteen minutes passed."

"That can't be," he began.

"It's been seven days. Almost to the minute, right?"

"No," said BK. Then he closed his eyes, presumably making his own count.

"What happened to the two of you?" the officer asked.

Neither answered.

The officer started to repeat her question.

"Nine days," BK interrupted. "That's how long it was for me."

"Are you certain?" asked the officer.

"Positive," BK said.

Then MK said, "Huh. I wonder why the difference."

But the problem had an easy enough answer. "I was down longer than you," her brother pointed out.

In frustration, the officer snarled, "But what in hell happened to you?"

The siblings glanced at one another.

Then they looked up, and they spoke the same words.

"Love happened," they said.

Elaborate graphs have been produced. Recorded testimonials and second-hand numbers have been plotted against axes that might be useful. Seventy thousand points in space and time will create pictures. For instance, there is a strong inverse correlation between the distance from the bomb and the duration spent being helpless. Spectators in the high seats generally woke that evening, while those closer to the field remained unconscious for days and often far longer. Being inside a restroom or otherwise shielded by concrete reduced the effects, but not as much as we might have guessed. Victims in the lowest seats, particularly those at the fifty-yard line, were slowest to wake. Yet their experiences pale next to the poor souls standing on the field itself—the band members and grounds crew, two teams and coaching staffs. Plus alumni and benefactors who had been given space on the sidelines. Those victims received the full onslaught of a very peculiar weapon, and several dozen died from brain hemorrhages, while others survived but have yet to open their eyes.

On the matter of correlations: There is a weaker but persistent positive correlation between how long someone was senseless and their perception of time.

Five days is the minimum "imaginary" time, while the record holder to date, if believed, is fifty-eight years.

Liquor consumption has no proven role in duration of helplessness or the depth of the experience. And despite rumors, cannabis had at most a minimal negative influence.

But judging by family reactions, genetic components can matter.

At this point, it bears stating that every number is just a number. Mathematical figures seem precise and cleanly rendered, yet in its nature, each number wants to mislead. Tidy graphs belay the scarcity of real data. Seventy thousand subjects were thrown into the same ad hoc experiment. No operative plans were made beforehand. No logistics were set in place. A college city with two major hospitals and minimal equipment for deep-brain analysis was trapped in the most unlikely scenario. Add to that the confounding facts of a wide-scale power outage and the substantial numbers of medical people—first responders and local physicians—trapped with the other victims inside the stadium. Also many key government people were struck down. The state's second-term governor was enjoying one of the luxury booths, which gave him valuable distance. But he was standing over the fourty-five-yard line and as a result was left unconscious for many days.

A genuine bomb would have left corpses and living people who knew what to do with corpses.

Broken bones and burns respond predictably to medical tools.

But what can be done with tens of thousands who are incapable of reacting to light or pain, or human voices, or any other reasonable treatment?

What city in this world could handle the crush of so many patients, each wrapped in a condition that doesn't resemble known comas or dream states?

The tragedy is still emerging.

What amazes us, writing from the midst of history, is the heroism of ordinary citizens facing an unexpected foe.

Case study:

SZ is a youthful fifty, a man who enjoyed prestige and responsibility in his lifelong profession. At the time of the attack, he was positioned high above the north fourty-five-yard line, apparently standing at the back of a luxury box. State troopers found him within the first hour, and because of his job and important friends, SZ was carried past other victims and placed inside a helicopter that whisked him to the state's premier neurological-care facility.

SZ was the first patient to receive full batteries of tests, including blood work and EEGs and several thorough PET scans.

As such, he enjoys a singular value among his peers.

SZ wasn't comatose or asleep, but characteristics of both states were observed. His body was limp, immune to mild pain and tickles. Loud sounds didn't rouse him. The voices of his wife and children had no visible effect. There was a persistent erection, but it wasn't associated with any normal REM sleep. If not for his arousal and rapid breathing, the man might have appeared dead, but the reality is that he was very far from death.

It bears repeating: Every victim's brain was at work. Trained athletes and world-class dancers make huge metabolic demands on their minds, but SZ's brain consumed more sugar and more oxygen than any brain studied before. No portion of his neurological system was at rest. Each breath supplied just enough air to maintain that fantastic storm of electricity, and because of fears that this middle-aged man would be overtaxed, SZ's breathing was augmented with an oxygen mask.

The treatment may or may not have had a role in his experience.

Frankly, nobody knows what his experience was.

For three weeks, the patient's condition held steady—no improvements or variations in his status. He was made comfortable, his body was hydrated, and once it was shown to be essential, he was fed sugar and proteins. (Starvation was and is an ongoing concern with every victim.) There was no reason to expect SZ to awaken, even after others from the same luxury box had opened their eyes. Three weeks had taught the doctors that they knew very little. After three weeks, even the most rational voice was speculating that a person didn't wake until he was ready.

Twenty-four days after the football game, SZ was ready.

Unless of course he just simply woke up.

His wife was in the room, and by chance, his oldest child. Like every other patient, SZ was lost to the world, attached machines measuring the quick vitals, and then he was back again. This was not the same as waking from deep sleep. His mind was alert, and then he and his body were alert in a different fashion. The only major physical problem were his atrophied muscles. According to a nurse present, SZ tried to sit up but couldn't. Then he spoke to his wife by name, and he smiled at the teenage daughter, and the girl responded by blurting out, "So who did you sleep with?"

By then, the world had learned what happened inside those raging minds—if not in detail, at least as a general rule.

Patients were meeting imaginary lovers and undergoing intense, soul-shaking affairs.

According the nurse, the girl's combative attitude startled SZ's wife.

"Honey," she said.

"I know you were cheating on Mom," the girl said.

SZ tried again to sit up.

The nurse attempted to help him.

"Get your hands off my father," the girl shouted.

"Leave us, please," the wife begged.

Standing in the hallway, the nurse overheard portions of a very difficult conversation. Her sense was that the girl was only voicing her mother's deepest concerns. For years, there had been stories of infidelity involving this very important man. But rumors didn't matter as much as the certainty that his mind—struck helpless by a terrorist attack—was happily engaged in a relationship that had no connection to real people and genuine events.

Beds were still at a premium at that stage in the crisis.

SZ was discharged as quickly as possible, and after several days of rest, appeared in public. His family stood beside him when he thanked the state troopers and hospital and the many subordinates who did his job in very trying times. Every observer was struck by the man's graciousness and his smile. There are people with famous smiles, and

SZ's was one of those. But the expression was different than before. The audience saw a transformative joy, not only in how he grinned but how that joy seemed to make him lighter and younger than any man in his fifties should be.

The rumors had already begun by then. Which makes it doubly disappointing that we don't have SZ's account about his time as an invalid. Yet the patients are rarely willing to speak about these personal experiences, and our subject was even more circumspect than the norm.

Whispers claimed that he lived twenty years in as many days.

That would put him at the high end of the charts.

Voices that might know the story claim that SZ enjoyed a torrid affair with a living actress—that is, an imaginary version of an Academy Award winner. But that is the kind of rumor that spreads. Because it is compelling and obvious, and a portion of those who are doing the telling wish they could have dreamed about sleeping with a woman like that.

Another story is that SZ had a twenty-year relationship with a youngster. The girl was only eleven at the beginning, and by the end, the dreaming man was sleeping with her as well as his various daughters.

That is the kind of story told by enemies and believed by only a few of them. Yet from what is known, pedophilia is unlikely but never impossible.

A third version exists. There was a large Christmas party where SZ had one drink too many and then confided to the wrong person. He claimed that the woman he loved for twenty-one imaginary years was as exotic and beautiful as any woman could be. But there was more than just that one woman in the other realm. He had lived inside a fully realized world, sharp and honest. A man who had never built anything with his hands built the house where he and his common-law wife lived together. They had several children. SZ mentioned names and grieved that he didn't have pictures of their little ones. He was that proud of them. Actual specifics were few, but the witness had the impression that this nonexistent mother and family lived in another age, perhaps inside a fantasy world—a world of grand beauty where everybody shared a crushing, relentless poverty.

SZ's wife filed for divorce shortly after New Year's.

He didn't contest her when she took their three children.

Rumors of depression seem to be untrue, but those same rumors led to talk about removing him from his post. SZ didn't give anyone that chance. He resigned on a Friday afternoon, slipping out of his office and then out of the country. The last credible sighting came from the border of Uganda and South Sudan. A white man matching SZ's description was seen walking alone into the bush, wearing tattered clothes and an enormous smile that washed away his miserable circumstances.

Certain categories make easy statistics, and perhaps these numbers have real significance.

But statistics are a game for bolder souls than ours.

Yes, there has been a strong rise in separations and divorces. The largest upticks come from males married for seven to twelve years and whose spouses weren't affected. And inside that group, the most susceptible are young men who experienced only a year or two of pernicious romance. (PR is the latest term for the condition. Will it last? Who knows?) Perhaps this says something about human nature. You spend two years with the girl of your dreams, and that's both too long and too short. Coming back into the old world, you look at your legal mate as an embarrassment or disappointment, or boring. Because your dream mate and you were still fresh to each other, and everything ended too soon.

Couples that collapsed together are less likely to divorce. Though their numbers are still higher than normal, and substantially so.

Older couples are most resilient.

Indeed, if a husband and wife fell into a stupor for just a few hours, and if they woke at nearly the same time, they often use the event as a bonding agent, revitalizing marriages that perhaps weren't as strong as they might have been.

Books are being written on the psychological effects.

Careers and entire new industries are being nourished.

One category that receives remarkably little attention: The effects on children and young teenagers. From what has been observed, young children always experienced a love affair, but non-sexual and with a parental figure. In their dream, some disaster had swept away life as they knew it, and they found an adoptive adult who led them through a series of great adventures, sometimes spanning decades of life and growth.

Those children are as profoundly changed as anyone. "Baby adults," they have been dubbed by observers and the occasional news feature.

And what other changes have been wrought?

Today, several thousand patients remain scattered in various facilities. They demand an expensive level of care, and if they don't wake in the next few months, their bodies will require new and aggressive interventions. And there are the social ramifications to a world making ready for the next attack—even if the first attack wasn't terroristic in nature. The health industry is devising huge, largely unworkable plans in case crowds and entire cities are rendered helpless. Billions are being spent on facilities that will wait in stasis for the next wave of casualties, giving us the chance to study them in detail. And there is the simple, relentless problem that comes from one difficult evening in October: Tens of thousands of people are awake today, dealing with lives that were never lived, and from all accounts those other lives seem to be as genuine and as thoroughly recalled as any.

How can so much human experience, sitting outside normal life, not have a significant impact on all of us?

What ideas did our neighbors and friends bring back from the other world?

And how will the echo of romance play, now and for the next thousand years?

Case study:

EL is a physical therapy major and a member of the football trainer's corp. That's why she was standing near the twenty-five-yard line, fully exposed to the blast. Among her peers, EL has various distinctions. As a patient, she was cared for at home by her mother and stepfather. That wasn't particularly unusual. There was a rampant shortage of hospital beds, particularly in those first three months, and many families took up the burden. But EL was a different kind of patient. Everyone had elevated breathing rates, but she was at the high end of the continuum. Perhaps youth and physical fitness made that possible. Or there were random or unknown factors. What is known is that she spent seventeen weeks in her own bed, cared for by people who had the resources and energy to meet her extraordinary needs. EL sounded like a sprinter when she breathed. Her mouth and nostrils became chapped, and she lost weight despite constant feedings through IVs, and later, tubes pushed down her throat. Twenty pounds evaporated from a frame that didn't enter that state overweight, and just before she woke, EL's mother was considering transferring her to an expensive care facility.

But her daughter woke before she starved. Perhaps because her body was suffering, it has been suggested. But only a handful of cases resemble hers, and those patients emerged long before the body failed.

Another distinction is that EL is easily the most forthcoming about her case. She began blogging immediately. The wasted body wouldn't let her sit up, but she wrote her first entries on her back, on a tablet held by her dutiful mother.

One might expect that her seventeen weeks would translate to an impressive stretch of illusionary years. But that isn't the case at all. EL felt that only nine years had passed, which again puts her at the tip of a bell curve. And where most dream lovers were idealized, hers seems to have been a more fully rounded individual.

Heather was the lover's name.

Is her name.

She was an older woman, beautiful and possessive and sometimes cruel, at least in an emotional sense. EL writes that she and Heather fought often and about every possible topic. They lived together for seven years, off and on. EL was working as a trainer for the Minnesota Vikings, and her lover held and lost an assortment of jobs.

In her blogs, EL duplicates long stretches of dialogue.

Of course their authenticity can't be determined. But EL's words match the tone and vocabulary that she prefers, and her lover is nothing if not consistent.

EL loved Heather despite or because of the flaws.

She loves her now.

This is perhaps the most intriguing and potentially disturbing part of this case: Awake again, EL is using every spare moment of her life to explain what happened to her inside a dream. And she claims that she does this because Heather is real, and Heather returned to this world with her. There is a second mind, vivid and pissed, smoldering inside a bored skull.

Subsequent PET scans have shown interesting abnormalities.

And EL still consumes more food than before, feeding a mind that insists on running faster than average.

Everyone with an interest in the outcome is watching, wondering if and how the parasite will try to take hold of its host.

Speculation is easy, and done properly, calm speculation might help our adaptations to the ongoing challenges.

But we continue to dismiss the terrorism theory, and for good reasons. What political movement has the requisite technical skills? Whatever the device's source, it was a high-end technology wielding powers born out of the most rarefied strata of theory, and these tools were used in a very unterroristic fashion. Few deaths. No claim of credit. Seventy thousand cases of love-sick revery, and no second attack either.

But that leaves a very important question:

Who are the reasonable suspects?

Exclude one word from that question, and quite a lot becomes possible.

Foreign governments were testing a new weapon.

Or perhaps our own government was.

A small, portable device that drops thousands into a helpless state. That would be an excellent way to cripple your enemy while leaving his infrastructure intact. That is an unreasonable scenario with considerable appeal. But the first complaint is to point out the scope of the test and the dozens dead. Wouldn't that bring too much notoriety? Unless that was the goal, of course. An unexpected nightmare delivered to the unwary world. But if this was and is an experimental weapon, then there is a slightly less unlikely explanation.

We call it the Castle Bravo scenario.

Castle Bravo was one of the first thermonuclear tests in the Pacific. The bomb's yield was two-and-a-half times larger than predicted, and the blast and fallout effects caused years of misery.

Perhaps our tragedy was the result of similar mistakes.

But if a government agency isn't to blame, then who?

A cult, perhaps. Although that perches close to the terrorist assumptions, with the added problem that no known cult carries any interest in pushing thousands into the arms of imaginary lovers.

Perhaps a major corporation was testing a new product, and its calculations were a thousandfold wrong.

Unlikely, but not impossible.

Even less likely explanations include aliens operating our midst, time travelers from some far human/machine future, and the utterly random hand of some capricious or incompetent god.

And waiting beyond the impossible:

The unthinkable.

Case study:

Tenured professors are allowed to purchase season tickets, though they are relegated to some famously poor locations. BB and his wife had seats high in the southwestern portion of the stadium. These were fit people but far from young. They left for the restrooms before the first half ended, and they were slowly climbing the steps when the stadium fell into darkness. Probably neither noticed the helmet and golf cart stopping in the middle of the field. BB does recall his wife hesitating in the gloom above him. He speaks affectionately about touching her back, trying to reassure her with his presence, and then came the flash that transported him to another world where he lived and loved for three alien days—long days which would translate to perhaps two weeks by the human count, he estimates.

To an accomplished physicist, that alternate world appeared perfectly credible.

Twenty-three minutes after the blast, BB woke to find himself lying on top of his wife. To his horror, he realized that she had fallen hard, driven in part by his own body. Her forehead sharp struck the edge of a concrete step. BB tended to the bloody wound as best he could, and then this man in his late seventies tried to lift his wife, and failed, before screaming as loudly as he could, begging for anyone's help.

Sitting nearby were a brother and sister, alert and conversing with one campus police officer. All three came to the rescue, and despite his own head wound, the brother carried the dying woman across other bodies and out into the nearest parking lot. But the medical personnel were elsewhere, lucid or otherwise, and this spouse of fifty-eight years died in the back of a useless ambulance.

BB's subsequent depression was prolonged and useful.

Two months after the funeral, he began working on an explanation for his wife's murder and the transformation of so many innocent lives. Those efforts led to a series of dense, harshly reasoned papers that have mostly gone unpublished. But the professional indifference hasn't kept his conclusions from being shared by others, both within his field and far beyond.

BB claims that what happened isn't possible. Not according to natural laws, and not according to any compilation of wild hypotheses.

Impossibility is itself a clue, says BB.

He has written nothing about his fictional love affair, but the alien world is a different subject. Thoroughly rendered, complete with estimates of size and mass, apparent history and harsh climate, he argues that the world was too intricate and perfect for even an expert to dream up. That means that his vision had to be the work of another mind, a much more competent and relentless mind. According to the old professor, each of us exists inside the dreams of someone greater, and what happened on that October evening was an accident, a sorry mistake.

The universe is a cosmic fiction.

That fiction is run by mathematics and vast, unseen machines.

Some tiny piece of the machinery failed. Which must happen from time to time, as every device has its limits.

BB argues that there was no bomb or other device inside that football helmet. The golf cart failed because of the initial surge of uninvited energies, and like a fuse popping inside a circuit box, the event came and went quickly enough. But there was leakage from the higher mind, and the professor has both equations and options for experiments that might someday prove him right.

As mentioned, BB has not published these results in any responsible journal.

Some of his peers want him to retire finally.

But the old man refuses. He likes to teach and do research. Those are the only blessings left for him, now that his wife is dead. But he remains confident that the woman lives on, probably somewhere in the higher mind, and death will come soon enough, freeing him for a long, joyous chase.

What constitutes reasonable answers?

We can't say. Months of study and endless discussion has left us with no clear options. But we have cobbled together a variety of stories that capture the elements of what we consider workable, sane explanations.

Remember the reported scent of perfume.

Maybe that's a key.

And the fifty-yard line too.

The incident was devised as a study, and the football field supplied a workable transect. Again, think of Castle Bravo. Consider the possibility that the effects far outweighed every projection. The EMP blast wasn't the first stage. The incident began when someone released a powerful chemical into the atmosphere. The chemical came from the giant helmet or from the hose being towed along, and it migrated inside everyone, brought to the lungs and blood where it had powerful hallucinogenic effects. Perhaps the electrical jolt was meant to height the drug's effects, or it was a substantial malfunction in an untested system.

The culprit here would be a major pharmaceutical corporation or a bioengineering start-up.

What was being tested was a genuine love potion.

Again, think of the nuclear blast that worked too well.

The event was meant to be both an experiment and a social event, and only the people on the field should have been infected.

Horrified by the aftermath, the guilty parties have destroyed their work and gone into hiding.

And no, we won't suggest that this is the genuine answer.

There is zero evidence backing up this story or any other. What we are proposing—indeed, what we insist is true—is that no answers will be forthcoming. Something large did happen. Nothing like it has happened before or since. And so it's reasonable, even responsible, to claim that we won't ever learn the truth, and that's the conundrum we need to deal with today.

Case study:

RL is a twenty-year-old woman. A cheerleader before the event, she woke only last week. After more than fifteen months of lying in various beds, in hospitals and then at home, she reports having spent fifty-eight years elsewhere.

Her fiance was her only visitor when she woke.

When told of the circumstances, RL appeared calm, even amused by what had to be unexpected news. This wasn't the shallow young woman who tumbled and waved pom-poms on the sidelines. She was composed, eerily so. The man whom she was supposed to marry was weeping, telling her about that awful night and the wild theories explaining what had happened. Tech wizards; evil governments; high minds; satanic spells. Then he grabbed one of her skeletal hands, describing how he had watched over her as much as anyone, that he always had been devoted and faithful, and he didn't care what she did inside that silly dream world. Dreams didn't matter. What mattered was that God had placed him into her life, here and now, giving him the strength to greet her return to what was real.

That rush of words and pent-up emotion finally ended.

A brief, wary silence followed.

And then the young/old woman laughed. It was a bittersweet sound— profound and hopeless, revealing the enormous gap between the two of them. Her fiance felt the hope draining out of him. His grip weakened. She retrieved her hand and then pointed at him, saying a few words in a language that he didn't know.

He eased away.

And then quietly, in the language she had barely used in half a century, she said, "The last thing I remember . . . "

"What is that?" he asked.

"His hand," she said.

"Whose hand?"

The laughter returned, even sadder.

Then she grabbed hold of herself, arms crossed on her starved chest, and she said, "My husband was behind me on the steps, in the dark. And he put his hand on my back, and just for a moment, just that last moment . . . I felt young again . . . "

ABOUT THE AUTHOR ⎯⎯⎯⎯⎯⎯⎯⎯⎯⎯⎯⎯⎯⎯⎯⎯

Robert Reed has had eleven novels published, starting with *The Leeshore* in 1987 and most recently with *The Well of Stars* in 2004. Since winning the first annual *L. Ron Hubbard Writers of the Future* contest in 1986 (under the pen name Robert Touzalin) and being a finalist for the John W. Campbell Award for best new writer in 1987, he has had over 200 shorter works published in a variety of magazines and anthologies. Eleven of those stories were published in his critically-acclaimed first collection, *The Dragons of Springplace,* in 1999. Twelve more stories appear in his second collection, *The Cuckoo's* Boys [2005]. In addition to his success in the U.S., Reed has also been published in the U.K., Russia, Japan, Spain and in France, where a second (French-language) collection of nine of his shorter works, *Chrysalide,* was released in 2002. Bob has had stories appear in at least one of the annual "Year's Best" anthologies in every year since 1992. Bob has received nominations for both the Nebula Award (nominated and voted upon by genre authors) and the Hugo Award (nominated and voted upon by fans), as well as numerous other literary awards (see Awards). He won his first Hugo Award for the 2006 novella "*A Billion Eves*". His most recent book is the *The Memory of Sky* (Prime Books, 2014).

The Long Haul
From the ANNALS OF TRANSPORTATION,
The Pacific Monthly, May 2009
KEN LIU

Twenty-five years ago on this day, the Hindenburg *crossed the Atlantic for the first time. Today, it will cross it for the last time. Six hundred times it has accomplished this feat, and in so doing it has covered the same distance as more than eight roundtrips to the Moon. Its perfect safety record is a testament to the ingenuity of the German people.*

There is always some sorrow in seeing a thing of beauty age, decline, and finally fade, no matter how gracefully it is done. But so long as men still sail the open skies, none shall forget the glory of the Hindenburg.
—John F. Kennedy, March 31, 1962, Berlin.

It was easy to see the zeppelins moored half a mile away from the terminal. They were a motley collection of about forty Peterbilts, Aereons, Macks, Zeppelins (both the real thing and the ones from Goodyear-Zeppelin), and Dongfengs, arranged around and with their noses tied to ten mooring masts, like crouching cats having tête-à-tête tea parties.

I went through customs at Lanzhou's Yantan Airport, and found Barry Icke's long-hauler, a gleaming silver Dongfeng Feimaotui—the model usually known in America, among the less-than-politically-correct society of zeppeliners, as the "Flying Chinaman"—at the farthest mooring mast. As soon as I saw it, I understood why he called it the *American Dragon*.

White clouds drifted in the dark mirror of the polished solar panels covering the upper half of the zeppelin like a turtle's shell. Large, waving American flags trailing red and blue flames and white stars were airbrushed onto each side of the elongated silver teardrop hull, which gradually tapered towards the back, ending in a cruciform tail striped in red, white, and blue. A pair of predatory, reptilian eyes were painted above the nose cone and a grinning mouth full of sharp teeth under it. A petite Chinese woman was suspended by ropes below the nose cone, painting over the blood-red tongue in the mouth with a brush.

Icke stood on the tarmac near the control cab, a small, round, glass-windowed bump protruding from the belly of the giant teardrop. Tall and broad-shouldered, his square face featured a tall, Roman nose and steady, brown eyes that stared out from under the visor of a Red Sox cap. He watched me approach, flicked his cigarette away, and nodded at me.

Icke had been one of the few to respond to my Internet forum ad asking if any of the long-haulers would be willing to take a writer for the *Pacific Monthly* on a haul. "I've read some of your articles," he had said. "You didn't sound too stupid." And then he invited me to come to Lanzhou.

After we strapped ourselves in, Icke weighed off the zeppelin—pumping compressed helium into the gasbags until the zeppelin's positive lift, minus the weight of the ship, the gas, us, and the cargo, was just about equal to zero. Now essentially "weightless," the long-hauler and all its cargo could have been lifted off the ground by a child.

When the control tower gave the signal, Icke pulled a lever that retracted the nose cone hook from the mooring mast and flipped a toggle to drop about a thousand pounds of water ballast into the ground tank below the ship. And just like that, we began to rise, steadily and in complete silence, as though we were riding up a skyscraper in a glass-walled elevator. Icke left the engines off. Unlike an airplane that needs the engines to generate forward thrust to be converted into lift, a zeppelin literally floats up, and engines didn't need to be turned on until we reached cruising height.

"This is the *American Dragon,* heading out to Sin City. See you next time, and watch out for those bears," Icke said into the radio. A few of the other zeppelins, like giant caterpillars on the ground below us, blinked their tail lights in acknowledgment.

Icke's Feimaotui is three hundred and two feet long, with a maximum diameter of eighty-four feet, giving it capacity for 1.12 million cubic feet of helium and a gross lift of thirty-six tons, of which about twenty-seven are available for cargo (this is comparable to the maximum usable cargo load for semis on the Interstates).

Its hull is formed from a rigid frame of rings and longitudinal girders made out of duratainium covered with composite skin. Inside, seventeen helium gasbags are secured to a central beam that runs from the nose to the tail of the ship, about a third of the way up from the bottom of the hull. At the bottom of the hull, immediately below the central beam and the gasbags, is an empty space that runs the length of the ship.

Most of this space is taken up by the cargo hold, the primary attraction of long-haulers for shippers. The immense space, many times the size of a plane's cargo bay, was perfect for irregularly shaped and bulky goods, like the wind generator turbine blades we were carrying.

Near the front of the ship, the cargo hold is partitioned from the crew quarters, which consists of a suite of apartment-like rooms opening off of a central corridor. The corridor ends by emerging from the hull into the control cab, the only place on the ship with windows to the outside. The Feimaotui is only a little bit longer and taller than a Boeing 747 (counting the tail), but far more voluminous and lighter.

The whole crew consisted of Icke and his wife, Yeling, the woman who was re-painting the grinning mouth on the zeppelin when I showed up. Husband-wife teams like theirs are popular on the transpacific long haul. Each of them would take six-hour shifts to fly the ship while the other slept. Yeling was in the back, sleeping through the takeoff. Like the ship itself, much of their marriage was made up of silence and empty space.

"Yeling and I are no more than thirty feet apart from each other just about every minute, but we only get to sleep in the same bed about once every seven days. You end up learning to have conversations in five-minute chunks separated by six-hour blocks of silence.

"Sometimes Yeling and I have an argument, and she'll have six hours to think of a comeback for something I said six hours earlier. That helps since her English isn't perfect, and she can use the time to look up words she needs. I'll wake up and she'll talk at me for five minutes and go to bed, and I'll have to spend the next six hours thinking about what she said. We've had arguments that went on for days and days this way."

Icke laughed. "In our marriage, sometimes you *have* to go to bed angry."

The control car was shaped like an airplane's cockpit, except that the windows slanted outward and down, so that you had an unobstructed view of the land and air below you.

Icke had covered his seat with a custom pattern: a topographical map of Alaska. In front of Icke's chair was a dashboard full of instruments and analog and mechanical controls. A small, gleaming gold statuette of a laughing, rotund bodhisattva was glued to the top of the dashboard. Next to it was the plush figure of Wally, the Green Monster of Fenway Park.

A plastic crate wedged into place between the two seats was filled with CDs: a mix of mandopop, country, classical, and some audio books. I flipped through them: Annie Dillard, Thoreau, Cormac McCarthy, *The Idiot's Guide to Grammar and Composition.*

Once we reached the cruising altitude of one thousand feet—freight zeppelins generally are restricted to a zone above pleasure airships, whose passengers prefer the view lower down, and far below the cruising height of airplanes—Icke started the electrical engines. A low hum, more felt than heard, told us that the four propellers mounted in indentations near the tail of the ship had begun to turn and push the ship forward.

"It never gets much louder than this," Icke said.

We drifted over the busy streets of Lanzhou. More than a thousand miles west of Beijing, this medium-sized industrial city was once the most polluted city in all of China due to its blocked air flow and petroleum processing plants. But it is now the center of China's wind turbine boom.

The air below us was filled with small and cheap airships that hauled passengers and freight on intra-city routes. They were a colorful bunch, a ragtag mix of blimps and small zeppelins, their hulls showing signs of make-shift repairs and *shanzhai* patches. (A blimp, unlike a zeppelin, has no rigid frame. Like a birthday balloon, its shape is maintained entirely by the pressure of the gas inside.) The ships were plastered all over with lurid advertisements for goods and services that sounded, with their strange English translations, frightening and tempting in equal measure. Icke told me that some of the ships we saw had bamboo frames.

Icke had flown as a union zeppeliner crewman for ten years on domestic routes before buying his own ship. The union pay was fine, but he didn't like working for someone else. He had wanted to buy a Goodyear-Zeppelin, designed and made one hundred percent in America. But he disliked bankers even more than Chinese airship companies, and decided that he would rather own a Dongfeng outright.

"Nothing good ever came from debt," he said. "I could have told you what was going to happen with all those mortgages last year."

After a while, he added, "My ship is mostly built in America, anyway. The Chinese can't make the duratainium for the girders and rings in the frame. They have to import it. I ship sheets of the alloy from Bethlehem, PA, to factories in China all the time."

The Feimaotui was a quirky ship, Icke explained. It was designed to be easy to maintain and repair rather than over-engineered to be durable the way American ships usually were. An American ship that malfunctioned had to be taken to the dealer for the sophisticated computers and proprietary diagnostic codes, but just about every component of the Feimaotui could be switched out and repaired in the field by a skilled mechanic. An American ship could practically fly itself most of the time, as the design philosophy was to automate as much as possible and minimize the chances of human error. The Feimaotui required a lot more out of the pilot, but it was also much more responsive and satisfying to fly.

"A man changes over time to be like his ship. I'd just fall asleep in a ship where the computer did everything." He gazed at the levers, sticks, wheels, toggles, pedals and sliders around him, reassuringly heavy, analog, and solid. "Typing on a keyboard is no way to fly a ship."

He wanted to own a fleet of these ships eventually. The goal was to graduate from owner-operator to just owner, when he and Yeling could start a family.

"Someday when we can just sit back and collect the checks, I'll get a Winnebago Aurora—the forty-thousand-cubic-feet model—and we and our kids will drift around all summer in Alaska and all winter in Brazil, eating nothing but the food we catch with our own hands. You haven't seen Alaska until you've seen it in an RV airship. We can go to places that not even snowmachines and seaplanes can get to, and hover over a lake that has never seen a man, not a soul around us for hundreds of miles."

Within seconds we were gliding over the broad, slow expanse of the Yellow River. Filled with silt, the muddy water below us was already beginning to take on its namesake color, which would deepen and grow even muddier over the next few hundred miles as it traveled through the Loess Plateau and picked up the silt deposited over the eons by wind.

Below us, small sightseeing blimps floated lazily over the river. The passengers huddled in the gondolas to look through the transparent floor at the sheepskin rafts drifting on the river below the same way Caribbean tourists looked through glass-bottom boats at the fish in the coral reef.

Icke throttled up and we began to accelerate north and east, largely following the course of the Yellow River, towards Inner Mongolia.

The Millennium Clean Energy Act is one of the few acts by the "clowns down in D.C." that Icke approved: "It gave me most of my business."

Originally designed as a way to protect domestic manufacturers against Chinese competition and to appease the environmental lobby, the law imposed a heavy tax on goods entering the United States based on the carbon footprint of the method of transportation (since the tax was not based on the goods' country-of-origin, it skirted the WTO rules against increased tariffs).

Combined with rising fuel costs, the law created a bonanza for zeppelin shippers. Within a few years, Chinese companies were churning out cheap zeppelins that sipped fuel and squeezed every last bit of advantage from solar power. Dongfengs became a common sight in American skies.

A long-haul zeppelin cannot compete with a 747 for lifting capacity or speed, but it wins hands down on fuel efficiency and carbon profile, and it's far faster than surface shipping. Going from Lanzhou to Las Vegas, like Icke and I were doing, would take about three to four weeks by surface shipping at the fastest: a couple days to go from Lanzhou to Shanghai by truck or train, about two weeks to cross the Pacific by ship, another day or so to truck from California to Las Vegas, and add in a week or so for loading, unloading, and sitting in customs. A direct airplane flight would get you there in a day, but the fuel cost and carbon tax at the border would make it uneconomical for many goods.

"Every time you have to load and unload and change the mode of transport, that's money lost to you," Icke said. "We are trucks that don't need highways, boats that don't need rivers, airplanes that don't need airports. If you can find a piece of flat land the size of a football field, that's enough for us. We can deliver door to door from a yurt in Mongolia to your apartment in New York—assuming your building has a mooring mast on top."

A typical zeppelin built in the last twenty years, cruising at one hundred ten mph, can make the sixty-nine-hundred-mile haul between Lanzhou and Las Vegas in about sixty-three hours. If it makes heavy use of solar power, as Icke's Feimaotui is designed to do, it can end up using less than a fraction of a percent of the fuel that a 747 would need to carry the same weight for the same distance. Plus, it has the advantage I'd mentioned of being more accommodating of bulky, irregularly-shaped loads.

Although we were making the transpacific long haul, most of our journey would be spent flying over land. The curvature of the Earth meant that the closest flight path between any two points on the globe followed a great circle that connected the two points and bisected the globe into two equal parts. From Lanzhou to Las Vegas, this meant that we would fly north and east over Inner Mongolia, Mongolia, Siberia, across the Bering Strait, and then fly east and south over Alaska, the Pacific Ocean off the coast of British Columbia, until we hit land again with Oregon, and finally reach the deserts of Nevada.

Below us, the vast city of Ordos, in Inner Mongolia, stretched out to the horizon, a megalopolis of shining steel and smooth glass, vast blocks of western-style houses and manicured gardens. The grid of new, wide streets was as empty as those in Pyongyang, and I could count the number of pedestrians on the fingers of one hand. Our height and open view made the scene take on the look of tilt-shift photographs, as though we were standing over a tabletop scale model of the city, with a few miniature cars and playing figurines scattered about the model.

Ordos is China's Alberta. There is coal here, some of the best, cleanest coal in the world. Ordos was planned in anticipation of an energy boom, but the construction itself became the boom. The more they spent on construction, the more it looked on paper like there was need for even more construction. So now there is this Xanadu, a ghost town from birth. On paper it is the second-richest place in China, per capita income just behind Shanghai.

As we flew over the center of Ordos, a panda rose up and hailed us. The panda's vehicle was a small blimp, painted olive green and carrying the English legend: "Aerial Transport Patrol, People's Republic of China." Icke slowed down and sent over the cargo manifests, the maintenance records, which the panda could cross-check against the international registry of cargo airships, and his journey log. After a few minutes, someone waved at us on from the window in the gondola of the blimp, and a Chinese voice told us over radio that we were free to move on.

"This is such a messed up country," Icke said. "They have the money to build something like Ordos, but have you been to Guangxi? It's near Vietnam, and outside the cities the people there are among the poorest in the world. They have nothing except the mud on the floor of their huts, and beautiful scenery and beautiful women."

Icke had met Yeling there, through a mail-order bride service. It was hard to meet women when you were in the air three hundred days of the year.

On the day of Icke's appointment, he was making a run through Nanning, the provincial capital, as part of a union crew picking up a shipment of star anise. He had the next day, a Saturday, off, and he traveled down to the introduction center a hundred kilometers outside Nanning to meet the girls whose pictures he had picked out and who had been bused in from the surrounding villages.

They had fifteen girls for him. They met in a village school house. Icke sat on a small stool at the front of the classroom with his back to the blackboard, and the girls were brought in to sit at the student desks, as though he was there to teach them.

Most of them knew some English, and he could talk to them for a little bit and mark down, on a chart, the three girls that he wanted to chat with one-on-one in private. The girls he didn't pick would wait around for the next Westerner customer to come and see them in another half hour.

"They say that some services would even let you try the girls out for a bit, like allow you to take them to a hotel for a night, but I don't believe that. Anyway, mine wasn't like that. We just talked. I didn't mark down three girls. Yeling was the only one I picked.

"I liked the way she looked. Her skin was so smooth, so young-looking, and I loved her hair, straight and black with a little curl at the end. She smelled like grass and rainwater. But I liked even more the way she acted with me: shy and very eager to please, something you don't see much in the women back home." He looked over at me as I took notes, and shrugged. "If you want to put a label on me and make the people who read what you write feel good about themselves., that's your choice. It doesn't make the label true."

I asked him if something felt wrong about the process, like shopping for a thing.

"I paid the service two thousand dollars, and gave her family another five thousand before I married her. Some people will not like that. They'll think something is not altogether right about the way I married her.

"But I know I'm happy when I'm with her. That's enough for me.

"By the time I met her, Yeling had already dropped out of high school. If I didn't meet her, she would not have gone on to college. She would not have become a lawyer or banker. She would not have gone to work in an office and come home to do yoga. That's the way the world is.

"Maybe she would have gone to Nanning to become a masseuse or bathhouse girl. Maybe she would have married an old peasant from the next village who she didn't even know just because he could give her family some money. Maybe she would have spent the rest of her life getting parasites from toiling in the rice paddies all day and bringing up children in a mud hut at night. And she would have looked like an old woman by thirty.

"How could that have been better?"

The language of the zeppeliners on the transpacific long haul, though officially English, is a mix of images and words from America and China. *Dao, knife, dough,* and *dollar* are used as interchangeable synonyms. Ursine imagery is applied to law enforcement agents along the route: a panda is a Chinese air patrol unit, and a polar bear Russian; in Alaska they are Kodiaks, and off the coast of BC they become whales; finally in America the ships have to deal with grizzlies. The bear's job is to make the life of the zeppeliner difficult: catching pilots who have been at the controls for more than six hours without switching off, who fly above or below regulation altitude, who mix hydrogen into the lift gas to achieve an extra edge in cargo capacity.

"Whales?" I asked Icke. How was whale a type of bear?

"Evolution," Icke said. "Darwin said that a race of bears swimming with their mouths open for water bugs may eventually evolve into whales." (I checked. This was true.)

Nothing changed as an electronic beep from the ship's GPS informed us that we crossed the international border between China and Mongolia somewhere in the desolate, dry plains of the Gobi below, dotted with sparse clumps of short, brittle grass.

Yeling came into the control cab to take over. Icke locked the controls and got up. In the small space at the back of the control cab, they spoke to each other for a bit in lowered voices, kissed, while I stared at the instrument panels, trying hard not to eavesdrop.

Every marriage had its own engine, with its own rhythm and fuel, its own language and control scheme, a quiet hum that kept everything moving. But the hum was so quiet that sometimes it was more felt than heard, and you had to listen for it if you didn't want to miss it.

Then Icke left and Yeling came forward to take the pilot's seat.

She looked at me. "There's a second bunk in the back if you want to park yourself a bit." Her English was accented but good, and you could hear traces of Icke's broad New England A's and non-rhoticity in some of the words.

I thanked her and told her that I wasn't sleepy yet.

She nodded and concentrated on flying the ship, her hands gripping the stick for the empennage—the elevators and rudders in the cruciform tail—and the wheel for the trim far more tightly than Icke had.

I stared at the empty, cold desert passing beneath us for a while, and then I asked her what she had been doing when I first showed up at the airport.

"Fixing the eyes of the ship. Barry likes to see the mouth all red and fierce, but the eyes are more important.

"A ship is a dragon, and dragons navigate by sight. One eye for the sky, another for the sea. A ship without eyes cannot see the coming storms and ride the changing winds. It won't see the underwater rocks near the shore and know the direction of land. A blind ship will sink."

An airship, she said, needed eyes even more than a ship on water. It moved so much faster and there were so many more things that could go wrong.

"Barry thinks it's enough to have these." She gestured towards the instrument panel before her: GPS, radar, radio, altimeter, gyroscope, compass. "But these things help Barry, not the ship. The ship itself needs to *see*.

"Barry thinks this is superstition, and he doesn't want me to do it. But I tell him that the ship looks more impressive for customers if he keeps the eyes freshly painted. That he thinks make sense."

Yeling told me that she had also crawled all over the hull of ship and traced out a pattern of oval dragon scales on the surface of the hull with tung oil. "It looks like the way the ice cracks in spring on a lake with good *fengshui*. A ship with a good coat of dragon scales won't ever be claimed by water."

The sky darkened and night fell. Beneath us was complete darkness, northern Mongolia and the Russian Far East being some of the least densely inhabited regions of the globe. Above us, stars, denser than I had ever seen, winked into existence. It felt as though we were drifting on the surface of a sea at night, the water around us filled with the glow of sea jellies, the way I remember when I used to swim at night in Long Island Sound off of the Connecticut coast.

"I think I'll sleep now," I said. She nodded, and then told me that I could microwave something for myself in the small galley behind the control cab, off to the side of the main corridor.

The galley was tiny, barely larger than a closet. There was a fridge, a microwave, a sink, and a small two-burner electric range. Everything was kept spotless. The pots and pans were neatly hung on the wall, and the dishes were stacked in a grid of cubbyholes and tied down with velcro straps. I ate quickly and then followed the sound of snores aft.

Icke had left the light on for me. In the windowless bedroom, the soft, warm glow and the wood-paneled walls were pleasant and induced sleep. Two bunks, one on top of another, hung against one wall of the small bedroom. Icke was asleep in the bottom one. In one corner of the room was a small vanity with a mirror, and pictures of Yeling's family were taped around the frame of the mirror.

It struck me then that this was Icke and Yeling's *home.* Icke had told me that they owned a house in western Massachusetts, but they spent only about a month out of the year there. Most of their meals were cooked and eaten in the *American Dragon,* and most of their dreams were dreamt here in this room, each alone in a bunk.

A poster of smiling children drawn in the style of Chinese folk art was on the wall next to the vanity, and framed pictures of Yeling and Icke together, smiling, filled the rest of the wall space. I looked through them: wedding, vacation, somewhere in a Chinese city, somewhere near a lake with snowy shores, each of them holding up a big fish.

I crawled into the top bunk, and between Icke's snores, I could hear the faint hum of the ship's engines, so faint that you almost missed it if you didn't listen for it.

I was more tired than I had realized, and slept through the rest of Yeling's shift as well as Icke's next shift. By the time I woke up, it was just after sunrise, and Yeling was again at the helm. We were deep in Russia, flying over the endless coniferous boreal forests of the heart of Siberia. Our course was now growing ever more easterly as we approached the tip of Siberia where it would meet Alaska across the Bering Sea.

She was listening to an audio book as I came into the control cab. She reached out to turn it off when she heard me, but I told her that it was all right.

It was a book about baseball, an explanation of the basic rules for non-fans. The particular section she was listening to dealt with the art of how to appreciate a stolen base.

Yeling stopped the book at the end of the chapter. I sipped a cup of coffee while we watched the sun rise higher and higher over the Siberian taiga, lighting up the lichen woodland dotted with bogs and pristine lakes still frozen over.

"I didn't understand the game when I first married Barry. We do not have baseball in China, especially not where I grew up.

"Sometimes, when Barry and I aren't working, when I stay up a bit during my shift to sit with him or on our days off, I want to talk about the games I played as a girl or a book I remember reading in school or a festival we had back home. But it's difficult.

"Even for a simple funny memory I wanted to share about the time my cousins and I made these new paper boats, I'd have to explain everything: the names of the paper boats we made, the rules for racing them, the festival that we were celebrating and what the custom for racing paper boats was about, the jobs and histories of the spirits for the festival, the names of the cousins and how we were related, and by then I'd forgotten what was the stupid little story I wanted to share.

"It was exhausting for both of us. I used to work hard to try to explain everything, but Barry would get tired, and he couldn't keep the Chinese names straight or even hear the difference between them. So I stopped.

"But I want to be able to talk to Barry. Where there is no language, people have to build language. Barry likes baseball. So I listen to this book and then we have something to talk about. He is happy when I can listen to or watch a baseball game with him and say a few words when I can follow what's happening."

Icke was at the helm for the northernmost leg of our journey, where we flew parallel to the Arctic Circle and just south of it. Day and night had lost their meaning as we flew into the extreme northern latitudes. I was already getting used to the six-hour-on, six-hour-off rhythm of their routine, and slowly synching my body's clock to theirs.

I asked Icke if he knew much about Yeling's family or spent much time with them.

"No. She sends some money back to them every couple of months. She's careful with the budget, and I know that anything she sends them she's worked for as hard as I did. I've had to work on her to get her to be a little more generous with herself, and to spend money on things that will make us happy right now. Every time we go to Vegas now she's willing to play some games with me and lose a little money, but she even has a budget for that.

"I don't get involved with her family. I figure that if she wanted out of her home and village so badly that she was willing to float away with a stranger in a bag of gas, then there's no need for me to become part of what she's left behind.

"I'm sure she also misses her family. How can she not? That's the way we all are, as far as I can see: we want that closeness from piling in all together and knowing everything about everyone and talking all in one breath, but we also want to run away by ourselves and be alone. Sometimes we want both at the same time. My mom wasn't much of a mom, and I haven't been home since I was sixteen. But even I can't say that I don't miss her sometimes.

"I give her space. If there's one thing the Chinese don't have, it's space. Yeling lived in a hut so full of people that she never even had her own blanket, and she couldn't remember a single hour when she was alone. Now we see each other for a few minutes every six hours, and she's learned how to fill up that space, all that free time, by herself. She's grown to like it. It's what she never had, growing up."

There is a lot of space in a zeppelin, I thought, idly. That space, filled with lighter-than-air helium, keeps the zeppelin afloat. A marriage also has a lot of space. What fills it to keep it afloat?

We watched the display of the aurora borealis outside the window in the northern skies as the ship raced towards Alaska.

I don't know how much time passed before I was jolted awake by a violent jerk. Before I knew what was going on, another sudden tilt of the ship threw me out of my bunk onto the floor. I rolled over, stumbled up, and made my way forward into the control cab by holding onto the walls.

"It's common to have storms in spring over the Bering Sea," Icke, who was supposed to be off shift and sleeping, was standing and holding onto the back of the pilot's chair. Yeling didn't bother to acknowledge me. Her knuckles were white from gripping the controls.

It was daytime, but other than the fact that there was some faint and murky light coming through the windows, it might as well have been the middle of the night. The wind, slamming freezing rain into the windows, made it impossible to see even the bottom of the hull as it curved up from the control cab to the nose cone. Billowing fog and cloud roiled around the ship, whipping past us faster than cars on the autobahns.

A sudden gust slammed into the side of the ship, and I was thrown onto the floor of the cab. Icke didn't even look over as he shouted at me, "Tie yourself down or get back to the bunk."

I got up and stood in the back right corner of the control cab, and used the webbing I found there to lash myself in place and out of the way.

Smoothly, as though they had practiced it, Yeling slipped out of the pilot chair and Icke slipped in. Yeling strapped herself into the passenger stool on the right. The line on one of the electronic screens that showed the ship's course by GPS indicated that we had been zigzagging around crazily. In fact, it was clear that although the throttle was on full and we were burning fuel as fast as an airplane, the wind was pushing us backwards relative to the ground.

It was all Icke could do to keep us pointed into the wind and minimize the cross-section we presented to the front of the storm. If we were pointed slightly at an angle to the wind, the wind would have grabbed us around the ship's peripatetic pivot point and spun us like an egg on its side, yawing out of control. The pivot point, the center of momentum around which a ship would move when an external force is applied, shifts and moves about an airship depending on the ship's configuration, mass, hull shape, speed, acceleration, wind direction, and angular momentum, among other factors, and a pilot kept a zeppelin straight in a storm like this by feel and instinct more than anything else.

Lightning flashed close by, so close that I was blinded for a moment. The thunder rumbled the ship and made my teeth rattle, as though the floor of the ship was the diaphragm of a subwoofer.

"She feels heavy," Icke said. "Ice must be building up on the hull. It actually doesn't feel nearly as heavy as I would have expected. The hull ought to be covered by a solid layer of ice now if the outside thermometer reading is right. But we are still losing altitude, and we can't go any lower. The waves are going to hit the ship. We can't duck under this storm. We'll have to climb over it."

Icke dropped more water ballast to lighten the ship, and tilted the elevators up. We shot straight up like a rocket. The *American Dragon's* elongated teardrop shape acted as a crude airfoil, and as the brutal Arctic wind rushed at us, we flew like an experimental model wing design in a wind tunnel.

Another bolt of lightning flashed, even closer and brighter than before. The rumble from the thunder hurt my eardrums, and for a while I could hear nothing.

Icke and Yeling shouted at each other, and Yeling shook her head and yelled again. Icke looked at her for a moment, nodded, and lifted his hands off the controls for a second. The ship jerked itself and twisted to the side as the wind took hold of it and began to turn it. Icke reached back to grab the controls as another bolt of lightning flashed. The interior lights went out as the lightning erased all shadows and lines and perspective, and the sound of the thunder knocked me off my feet and punched me hard in the ears. And I passed into complete darkness.

By the time I came to, I had missed the entire Alaskan leg of the journey.

Yeling, who had the helm, was playing a Chinese song through the speakers. It was dark outside, and a round, golden moon, almost full and as big as the moon I remember from my childhood, floated over the dark and invisible sea. I sat down next to Yeling and stared at it.

After the chorus, the singer, a woman with a mellow and smooth voice, began the next verse in English:

But why is the moon always fullest when we take leave of one another?
For us, there is sorrow, joy, parting, and meeting.
For the moon, there is shade, shine, waxing and waning.
It has never been possible to have it all.
All we can wish for is that we endure,
Though we are thousands of miles apart,
Yet we shall gaze upon the same moon, always lovely.

Yeling turned off the music and wiped her eyes with the back of her hand.

"She found a way out of the storm," she said. There was no need to ask who she meant. "She dodged that lightning at the last minute and found herself a hole in the storm to slip through. Sharp eyes. I knew it was a good idea to repaint the left eye, the one watching the sky, before we took off."

I watched the calm waters of the Pacific Ocean pass beneath us.

"In the storm, she shed her scales to make herself lighter."

I imagined the tung oil lines drawn on the ship's hull by Yeling, the lines etching the ice into dragon scales, which fell in large chunks into the frozen sea below.

"When I first married Barry, I did everything his way and nothing my way. When he was asleep, and I was flying the ship, I had a lot of time to think. I would think about my parents getting old and me not being there. I'd think about some recipe I wanted to ask my mother about, and she wasn't there. I asked myself all the time, *what have I done?*

"But even though I did everything his way, we used to argue all the time. Arguments that neither of us could understand and that went nowhere. And then I decided that I had to do something.

"I rearranged the way the pots were hung up in the galley and the way the dishes were stacked in the cabinets and the way the pictures were arranged in the bedroom and the way we stored life vests and shoes and blankets. I gave everything a better flow of *qi,* energy, and smoother *fengshui.* It might seem like a cramped and shabby place to some, but the ship now feels like our palace in the skies.

"Barry didn't even notice it. But, because of the *fengshui,* we didn't argue any more. Even during the storm, when things were so tense, we worked well together."

"Were you scared at all during the storm?" I asked.

Yeling bit her bottom lip, thinking about my question.

"When I first rode with Barry, when I didn't yet know him, I used to wake up and say, in Chinese, *who is this man with me in the sky?* That was the most I've ever been scared.

"But last night, when I was struggling with the ship and Barry came to help me, I wasn't scared at all. I thought, it's okay if we die now. I know this man. I know what I've done. I'm home."

"There was never any real danger from lightning," Icke said. "You knew that, right? The *American Dragon* is a giant Faraday cage. Even if the lightning had struck us, the charge would have stayed on the outside of the metal frame. We were in the safest place over that whole sea in that storm."

I brought up what Yeling had said, that the ship seemed to know where to go in the storm.

Icke shrugged. "Aerodynamics is a complex thing, and the ship moved the way physics told it to."

"But when you get your Aurora, you'll let her paint eyes on it?"

Icke nodded, as though I had asked a very stupid question.

Las Vegas, the diadem of the desert, spread out beneath, around, and above us.

Pleasure ships and mass-transit passenger zeppelins covered in flashing neon and gaudy giant flickering screens dotted the air over the Strip. Cargo carriers like us were constricted to a narrow lane parallel to the Strip with specific points where we were allowed to depart to land at the individual casinos.

"That's Laputa," Icke pointed above us, to a giant, puffy, baroque airship that seemed as big as the Venetian, which we were passing below and to the left. Lit from within, this newest and flashiest floating casino glowed like a giant red Chinese lantern in the sky. Air taxis rose from the Strip and floated towards it like fireflies.

We had dropped off the shipment of turbine blades with the wind farm owned by Caesars Palace outside the city, and now we were headed for Caesars itself. Comp rooms were one of the benefits of hauling cargo for a customer like that.

I saw, coming up behind the Mirage, the tall spire and blinking lights of the mooring mast in front of the Forum Shops. It was usually where the great luxury personal yachts of the high-stakes rollers moored, but tonight it was empty, and a transpacific long-haul Dongfeng Feimaotui, a Flying Chinaman named the *American Dragon,* was going to take it for its own.

"We'll play some games, and then go to our room," Icke said. He was talking to Yeling, who smiled back at him. This would be the first chance they had of sleeping on the same bed in a week. They had a full twenty-four hours, and then they'd take off for Kalispell, Montana, where they would pick up a shipment of buffalo bones for the long haul back to China.

I lay in bed in my Downtown hotel room thinking about the way the furniture in my bedroom was arranged, and imagined the flow of *qi* around the bed, the nightstands, the dresser. I missed the faint hum of the zeppelin's engines, so quiet that you had to listen hard to hear them.

I turned on the light and called my wife. "I'm not home yet. Soon."

[This story was inspired in many ways by John McPhee's Uncommon Carriers. *Some liberty has been taken with the physical geography of our world: a great circle flight path from Lanzhou to Las Vegas would not actually cross the city of Ordos.*

The lyrics of the song that Yeling plays come from a poem by the Song Dynasty poet Su Shi (1037-1101 A.D). It has remained a popular poem to set to music through the centuries since its composition.]

ABOUT THE AUTHOR

Ken Liu is an author and translator of speculative fiction, as well as a lawyer and programmer. A winner of the Nebula, Hugo, and World Fantasy Awards, he has been published in *The Magazine of Fantasy & Science Fiction, Asimov's, Analog, Clarkesworld, Lightspeed,* and *Strange Horizons,* among other places. He lives with his family near Boston, Massachusetts.

Ken's debut novel, *The Grace of Kings,* the first in a silkpunk epic fantasy series, will be published by Saga Press, Simon & Schuster's new genre fiction imprint, in April 2015. Saga will also publish a collection of his short stories.

Cody

PAT CADIGAN

"Common wisdom has it," said LaDene from where she was stretched out on the queen-sized bed, "that anyone with a tattoo on their face goes crazy within five years."

Cody paused in his examination of his jawline in the mirror over the desk to give her a look. "You see any tattoos on this example of manly beauty?"

"Can't see the moon from here, either. Or the TV remote," she added she sat up and looked around. Cody found it on the desk and tossed it to her. "Thanks. You know, carnies would call you a marked man."

"Carnies?" He gave a short laugh. "Don't tell me you threw over the bright lights of the midway to keep a low profile in budget accommodations."

"*Higher-end* budget accommodations." She put on the TV and began channel-surfing. "For the discerning yet financially savvy business traveler. Don't you ever read the brochures?"

He made a polite noise that was could have been yes or no and was neither. The hotspot that had come up over two hours ago was still there, midway between his chin and the point of his jaw, and as far as he could tell, it hadn't faded even a little. The medic had assured him there was nothing to worry about unless it started to spread and it hadn't. It wouldn't have bothered him except he hadn't had a hotspot in years. Rookies got hotspots.

The sudden recurrence could have been down to any number of things, the medic had said, the mostly likely being the attack of hayfever he had suffered on arrival. But he'd never had hayfever in his life, he'd told the medic. He'd never been to Kansas City in late August, she'd replied, chuckling.

Technically, he still hadn't. The airport was thirty miles north of the city and the car they'd sent had taken him to an industrial park about as far to the west on the Kansas side of the state line, which apparently ran right through the middle of town. The most he'd seen of Kansas City proper was a distant cluster of skyscrapers, briefly glimpsed through the tinted window as the driver negotiated a complicated interchange of highway ramps. After that it was generic highway scenery all the way to a generic suburban industrial park, full of angular, antiseptic office buildings surrounded by patches of green landscaped and manicured *in extremis,* some with a koi pond or a fountain. The access road meandered through it so much that Cody thought there had to be an extra mile of travel. Albeit a very pretty mile; perhaps it was so people coming and going could see at least in passing the flowers they didn't have time to stop and smell. Cody could have done without it. By the time they'd reached their destination, he had actually begun to feel carsick.

"Yo!" A pillow hit him in the head, making him jump. "And I thought *I* was vain," LaDene laughed. "Are you really that fascinating?"

"I was woolgathering," he said as he threw the pillow back at her. "Thinking, in case you don't know what that means."

"I know what it means," she said. "I also know you've got a hotspot. Unclench, honey, I've got one, too." She lifted her shirt and pointed at her navel.

"Oh, very funny."

"Oh, very for-real." She was up off the bed and had his face in her hands before he could say anything. "Ah, got it, right there." She patted his cheek and pulled up her shirt again, exposing her midriff. "Mine's hotter. Feel."

Her bellybutton was only inches away from his nose. Cody drew back and started to protest as she grabbed his hand and pressed it against her skin. His discomfort turned to surprise. "I sit corrected," he said, extricating himself from her grip. "Yours *is* hotter."

"Told you," she said, plumping down on the bed to stretch out again. "It's probably the ragweed and who knows what else in the air. Man, I *hate* KC this time of year."

"You've been here before?"

"I'm *from* here." She laughed at his surprised expression. "You couldn't tell?"

"How could I? We just met."

"I knew *you* weren't from around here, soon as I saw you. No antihistamines."

He chuckled a bit ruefully. "I thought I was dying of a head cold I caught on the plane."

She started to channel-surf again, then changed her mind and shut the TV off. "If you get cold symptoms a lot when you fly, it's probably an allergy."

"Oh?" He gave a short skeptical laugh. "Is there a lot of ragweed on airplanes?"

She shrugged. "Lots of other stuff—mold, dust, newsprint. Somebody's cheap cologne. Even expensive cologne."

"*Newsprint?*"

"Believe it or leave it. You know how if something exists, there's porn of it? Well, there's also someone allergic to it."

"Newsprint," Cody said again, still skeptical.

"If I'm lyin', I'm dyin.'" LaDene raised one hand solemnly, then let it fall. "Okay, that was fun. Now whaddaya wanna do?"

Cody leaned over and scooped the remote control up so he could turn the TV back on, mainly to forestall the possibility of her wanting to compare hotspots again. The screen lit up to show a dark-haired, olive-skinned woman speaking directly to the camera with an earnest sincerity that made his own brow furrow in sympathy.

" . . . found flayed and burned in a midtown Kansas City, Missouri parking garage have now positively been identified as August Fiore, AKA Little Augie Flowers, fifty-one, and Coral Oh, twenty-nine, of Liberty, Missouri. Fiore went missing two weeks ago from an FBI safe house where he was being held pending the start of the trial of Carmine Nesparini on racketeering charges. The FBI has steadfastly refused to comment on allegations that Fiore was Nesparini's personal 'master key' but sources close to the investigation say that Fiore's cooperation would have given authorities an unprecedented level of access to mob records.

"Fiore's attorneys refused to comment, except to say that they were unaware of any escape plans and had no knowledge of Fiore's whereabouts. Whether Fiore left the safe house voluntarily may never be known. FBI technicians are still working on the sabotaged surveillance system but experts believe there is little chance they can salvage enough data to be useful.

"Coral Oh's connection to Fiore still has not been established. Oh worked for the Kansas City Convention Bureau for fifteen years as an event coordinator, for the last three in a supervisory position. Co-workers described her as intelligent and well liked. She was last seen ten days ago in her office by two of her subordinates, who had been working late with her."

The woman was suddenly replaced by a video of a very young man who looked as if he hadn't slept for at least that long. The slightly wobbly graphic at the bottom of the screen said he was *Akule Velasquez.*"She told us to go home, she'd finish up," he said in a husky voice to someone just off-camera to the left. "We'd've stayed but she was all—" he made small shooing gestures with both hands. "'No, get outa here, I'll finish, bring me some fancy coffee tomorrow.' She was like that. I tried to stay anyway but she kept telling me no. I wish I hadn't listened."

The woman in the studio reappeared, looking more earnest and sincere than ever. "The mayor's office issued a statement saying that this unfortunate and tragic incident should not overshadow the fact that criminal activity in the area has been steadily declining for the past twelve months thanks to new policing initiatives—"

LaDene snatched the remote out of his hand and turned off the TV. "Well, that *wasn't* fun. Now what do you wanna do?"

"Hey, I was watching that." Cody reached for the remote but she threw it across the room where it bounced off the wall and fell neatly into a small waste basket.

"She shoots, she scores! A three-pointer, the crowd goes *wild!*" LaDene made crowd noises as he stalked over to retrieve the control. The impact had knocked the batteries out and it took him two tries to put them back in properly. "Oh, come *on*. What do you wanna scare the shit out of yourself for?"

But the news had moved on; now a man was standing near the edge of an empty swimming pool, blinking in bright sunlight as he talked about levels of chlorine. "Oh, well." Cody dropped the remote on the bed and sat down on the chair by desk again. "I wasn't trying to scare myself."

"Who *were* you trying to scare—me?"

"No. I just want to pay attention."

"Set a news alert on your phone." She was channel-surfing again. "It's probably all bullshit anyway. 'Little Augie Flowers,' for God's sake. Who goes around calling themselves 'Little Augie Flowers'? For a minute there, I thought they were talking about some old Grand Theft Auto module. 'Gay Tony Meets Little Augie Flowers, bullets will fly, heads will roll!' Oh, hey, I *love* this!" she added, sitting up suddenly.

Cody barely had to look at the screen to know what it was. "I've seen it." He rested an elbow on the desk and cupped his face in his hand. The hotspot was still there. "Several times."

"So have I but I like to watch it whenever it's on. That guy's *so cool*."

"He is?" If he didn't leave the goddam hotspot alone, he told himself, it was never going to fade. He shifted so he was leaning the upper part of his cheek against his hand; as if it had a will of its own, his thumb slid down to feel his jawline. Annoyed with himself, he straightened up, grabbed the TV listings off the desk and paged through them without seeing anything.

"Okay, he's all wrong and he probably knew it," LaDene was saying. She punched the pillows behind her into a more supportive position for her lower back and casually folded her legs into a half-lotus, making Cody wince. "But so what? The whole movie's wrong."

"Well, it's a pretty old movie," he said, shrugging.

"Not *that* old. Not *ancient*."

"No, but BCI didn't even exist when this came out and people were still using floppy disks. This big." He held his hands three feet apart. She gave him a look and he moved them so they were only a foot apart. "Okay, *this* big. TVs were dumb terminals and a cloud was a fluffy white thing in the sky. So the idea of people giving up memories to store data in their brains—"

LaDene waved one hand dismissively. "I was referring to the cell phones."

He frowned. "What cell phones?"

"Exactly!" She laughed. "How the *hell* did they miss *cell phones?*"

As if on cue, there was a sound like a ray-gun in a scifi movie and the ring on her right hand lit up with tiny flashing lights. She cocked her head, listening, then bounced off the bed. "My ride's here. See you around—" Her grin was sheepish.

"Cody," he said.

"Right." She paused, one eyebrow raised, the other down low, something Cody had never been able to manage no matter how hard he'd tried. "That's really your name."

"LaDene's really yours?" he said evenly.

"I grew up in Tonganoxie, Kansas. Of *course* it's really my name."

The two statements seemed unrelated to him but he nodded anyway. She pulled her suitcase out of the closet, extended the handle and then paused again, one hand on the doorknob. "Where are *you* from?"

"I used to know but I rented that out for a database back-up."

He heard her laughing all the way down the hall.

He ate alone in the dining room. The waitress gave him a table by a window that made the most of the hotel's location atop a rocky promontory, so he could enjoy his chicken Caesar salad with a scenic view of three other hotels and the six-lane highway running between them.

While it may not have been classic postcard material, he had to admit the view was actually rather nice. Kansas wasn't as flat as most people seemed to think, at least not in this locale. Here the landscape was gently rolling, punctuated by flat stretches usually occupied by malls or apartment complexes. In the distance, he could see the top of a mall that had to be the size of an airplane hangar and, not far from that, a crane surrounded by a framework suggesting future apartments or condos.

But it was the highway that drew his eye more than anything. He couldn't remember the last time he had seen so many private cars. Well, the travel agent had told him this was one of the last bastions of the autonomous commuter. Cody couldn't imagine what it was like to spend an hour or more of every weekday driving. He'd had a license himself once, but only briefly. After it had expired, he hadn't bothered renewing it and didn't miss it.

Perhaps if he were driving now, he'd be too busy to keep worrying at that stupid hotspot. Annoyed with himself, he pulled the complimentary library up on the table-top and checked out the local newspaper.

The waitress tried to talk him into dessert every time she refilled his iced tea. After his third glass, he swiped his keycard through the table-top reader, left an overly generous cash tip, and went back up to the room. It seemed a lot emptier now that LaDene was gone. Even the pillows she had piled against the headboard looked forlorn. He hadn't been thrilled to find her there when he'd checked in. She had apologized profusely—some kind of travel-plan fiasco. Having been through a few of those himself, he was sympathetic. As it turned out, she'd been good company—better than he'd realized. His newly-recovered privacy felt lonely.

He stretched out in the place where she had been and put the TV on again. It was only one night, and as LaDene had pointed out, this was a higher-end budget hotel. The complimentary coffee service was a drip pot with pouches of a gourmet blend rather than merely a kettle and two envelopes of instant. The minibar was well stocked with a wide variety of refreshments and if all of it cost ten times what it would in a grocery store, at least the cans of mixed nuts were a bit larger than average.

And then there was the television. Twenty channels including sports and movies, not counting the on-demand you had to pay extra for. Most places didn't offer half that. Maybe it was their way of compensating people like him, who were stuck there without a car.

Although that wasn't *quite* true. A chat with the desk clerk had revealed that they were less than a mile away from what she referred to as a shopping village, which he quickly figured out was a clever euphemism for strip mall. It wasn't much, she'd said in a politely cautioning tone meant to discourage any ideas of a foray on foot—a discount electronics outlet, a hardware store, an indoor playground, and three fast-food joints. Cody decided he could live without seeing it.

"Good choice," the clerk had said approvingly. "Because you'd be taking your life in your hands—no sidewalks."

"No sidewalks where?" he'd asked, puzzled.

"Between here and the shopping village."

"Then where do people walk?"

"They don't. People have to drive to get out here. They park, do whatever they came to do, then drive home again. I mean, you don't walk on the interstate, either."

Cody had been tempted to ask if she ever went for walks herself and if so, where, but decided against it. She was twenty-two at most, about to go from merely young and pretty to eye-catching as the last of her adolescent puppy-fat disappeared. She might have thought he was hitting on her and if he were honest, he might have had a hard time denying it.

He found a 24-hour news channel, turned the volume down to a murmur, and then used the remote to shut off the lights.

The next thing he knew, someone was sitting on his chest.

He could see nothing in the dark except a darker shadow looming over him, blocking out the flickering light from the television. He tried to yell but his mouth refused to open and he only made a sort of high-pitched grunt. Something pressed hard against his windpipe as whoever had him pinned bent over to speak close to his ear.

"You want to lie very still and not make a sound," said a male voice, just above a whisper. "Then do exactly what I tell you. I don't want to hurt you. I'm not here to hurt you. But I will if I have to."

His heart was beating hard and fast, as if it were trying to pound its way out of his chest. The pressure on his windpipe eased but didn't go away entirely. He swallowed, wincing.

As the man straightened up, Cody made out long graying hair, possibly tied back, and thick-framed glasses. "First, don't try to open your mouth. You're short-circuited and you'll only give yourself a headache. Once I know you're gonna behave yourself, I'll consider letting you chew gum."

He tried to make a conciliatory noise; the pressure on his windpipe increased again.

"I *said*, don't make a sound."

Cody sucked air through his nose, feeling himself jerk helplessly as his body fought to cough even though his mouth wouldn't open. His throat clenched, knotted, and tried to turn itself inside out. Then all at once, his mouth did open, just long enough for him to let out a few explosive coughs before his jaw snapped shut again.

"Better?"

Cody nodded, breathing in hungrily through his nose.

"You understand now to do *exactly* what I say?"

He nodded again.

"After I let you up, you're gonna change your clothes. Then you'll be taken out of here in a wheelchair. You're gonna sit quiet and stare at your lap. You're not gonna look up. If anyone speaks to you, you'll act like you didn't hear anything. There's a van waiting out front. You'll be put into it, chair and all, and we'll drive away.

"Now, it's important you remember everything I just said and do exactly that because an associate of mine is having a chat with the night clerk. Nice older man, a grandfather, in fact. If, while we pass through the lobby, he should get the idea that you need help, my associate will hurt him, badly. Unlike me, my associate doesn't mind hurting anyone. You don't want to harm innocent bystanders, do you."

Cody shook his head from side to side.

"Very good. Now, when I let you up, you're going to strip naked and put on what I've brought for you."

The man climbed off him and stood back. Cody moved more slowly as he slid over to the edge of the bed and began to unbutton his shirt with shaky fingers.

"A little faster, please," the man said, staring at the television with his arms folded. Cody wanted to comply but he was so unsteady he was off-balance even sitting down. He shoved his trousers down, extricating his ankles one at a time, socks and all. Next to him was a small neat pile of clothing folded into squares. Trembling, he picked up the top item; it was a hospital gown.

"Ties in back," the man said, casually matter of fact, as if he were remarking on the weather. He never looked away from the television.

Cody couldn't have tied his shoelaces. He decided it didn't matter; the second item was a bathrobe. He put it on sitting down, then pushed himself carefully to his feet.

The man turned from the television to give him an up-and-down.

"I told you to strip *naked*. Lose the tidy-whiteys."

Cody fell over on the bed in the rush to gets his shorts off. The man waited with a put-upon air till he was done, then took hold of his upper arm and pulled him up. Cody winced; his grip was unnaturally strong, well out of proportion for a slight, older man almost a head shorter than he was.

The man waiting in the hallway with the wheelchair was a lot taller and huskier, dressed in a dark blue coverall; there was a patch on his left breast pocket showing a picture of a first-aid kit and the words County EMS. He said nothing as Cody stumbled over the foot-rests and fell into the seat. The frame was lightweight and all the wheels were small. The gray-haired man bent over him and Cody saw he was wearing the same uniform.

"You remember what I told you," he said and Cody noticed how little his rather pasty face moved, as if he'd Botoxed it into submission. And out here, up close and personal in much brighter light, the gray hair looked like a wig, ponytail and all. "Think of that poor man's family. Whether he goes home when his shift is over is all down to you." He stared into Cody's eyes as if he expected to see some response there, then chuckled and patted his cheek. "And seriously, relax your jaw. I'm not kidding about the headache." Cody started to rub the side of his face but the man caught his hand and put it firmly in his lap. "You don't move till we're out of here. Can you manage that or should I help you?"

Cody bowed his head.

"By George, I think he's got it."

Despite the carpeting, the ride was bumpy—the chair had a wobbly wheel, like every supermarket shopping cart Cody had ever used. But he stared fixedly at the slightly threadbare material covering his knees as they went down in the elevator. When they reached the lobby, he bowed his head a little more and squeezed his eyes shut, afraid they'd kill the desk clerk anyway. Having seen their faces, he'd be able to give a description to the police, which didn't bode well for his survival.

Or for his own.

The thought was a cold electric shock running down his back as the automatic doors hummed open in front of him. He heard the desk clerk tell someone to have a good night and a woman responded *I surely will, you too!* in a cheerful, friendly tone.

Then he was outside, rattling toward a white van with the same County EMS painted on the open side door. A tall woman waited beside a wheelchair lift.

• • •

Cody had no idea how long they had been on the road before the gray-haired man reached over and touched something to a spot under his cheekbone near the hinge of his jaw. He was in the middle of a huge yawn almost before it registered on him that he could open his mouth again. The muscles on either side of his face felt overworked and sore, including some he had never actually known were there. He worked his jaw for a while, knowing the gray-haired man was watching him and trying not to care.

He was sitting in a fold-down seat on Cody's right, facing backwards. The husky guy had anchored the wheelchair against a padded backstop and strapped him in before taking the seat on his left. The tall woman was up front, next to the driver. The woman who had been talking to the night clerk was behind him, along with at least one other person he had neither seen nor heard and who apparently wanted to keep it that way. Unbidden, the idea came to him that it was LaDene; he put it quickly out of his mind. Paranoia wasn't going to help.

Cody rested his head against the backstop and closed his eyes, wondering if he actually could go to sleep. Under the circumstances, there wasn't anything else he could do. But his mind was as alert as if he were in the middle of a busy day, which he supposed he was. Pretending to be asleep was a waste of time, thanks to the hospital gown; he figured they'd souped it up to where it could practically read his mood.

He opened his eyes and saw the gray-haired man watching him. Almost reflexively, he was overwhelmed by another huge yawn.

"You know the situation," the gray-haired man said, when his yawn had passed.

Cody nodded. "And *you* know I don't know anything."

"You don't have to," the man said.

"I'm a courier," Cody added. "Even if I wanted to, I couldn't access anything—"

"We know," the other man said, sounding short.

"—I have no knowledge of the quantity or nature of any data—"

"Yes, we're aware—"

"—nor am I responsible if any attempts at access cause damage, in whole or in part, to that data or any hardware or software—"

"We *already* know that—" He was openly impatient now.

"—my safe return cannot not indemnify any party against criminal charges of kidnapping and false imprisonment," Cody went on, trying not to enjoy the man's irritation too much as he talked over him, "which are brought by the state and not by companies or individuals." He said the last couple of words through another yawn. "Whew. Excuse me.

I'm obligated by the terms of my employment to apprise you of those facts. I can also write it all down for you and sign it."

The man on his left perked up. "Seriously? Like, if you don't say all that, they'd fire you?" Cody nodded. The man thought it over for a second. "What if we all claimed you didn't?"

"Shut up," the gray-haired man said, raising his voice.

Cody pretended not to hear. "I'd tell them I did."

"And they'd just believe you?"

"I'm level-four bonded," Cody replied. "On the job, I'm permanently under oath. If I lie, it's perjury."

"Shut your face or I'll shut it for you," said the gray-haired man, triggering Cody's urge to yawn again. The man waited till he was done, then added: "Anything else in the way of legal disclaimers? Health warnings? Household hints?"

Cody gave his head a quick shake and dropped his gaze to his lap. They traveled in silence for some unmeasured amount of time. Abruptly, the man on his left straightened up. "I just can't get my head around anyone just taking this guy's word about anything," he blurted.

"When we get where we're going, you can look it up on Wikipedia," the gray-haired man said acidly. "Last warning—shut your mouth."

Cody hardly dared to look up after that; whenever he did, the gray-haired man always seemed to be watching him. He stared into the darkness, listening to the thrum of the tires and air rushing past. No one said anything about a rest stop and he doubted there was any point in asking—the gray-haired guy would probably offer him a Coke bottle. He shifted in the chair and concentrated on making himself relax. He had said what he had to say; his best course of action now was to avoid further antagonizing the gray-haired man.

It was just starting to grow lighter outside when he finally dozed off.

He woke from an unpleasant dream of many hands grabbing at him to find the big man unstrapping the chair while the gray-haired man poked his shoulder, telling him over and over to wake up. Exhaustion overwhelmed him, weighed him down so that just getting his eyes open was a major effort and when he finally did, they wouldn't stay open for longer than half a second. Then he was wheeled onto the lift and the humid heat that had not yet permeated the van's still-cool interior hit him in the face and seemed to suck all the air from his lungs.

Groggy, almost gasping, he noticed the van was now green and brown, bearing the logo of a large national rental company. More unsettling was seeing that they were in a parking garage. The gray-haired man leaned over him, looking pastier and more impassive than ever. "This will be less unpleasant if we don't have to force you. Not that it's a party. But if I have to short your circuits, it'll only be more of an ordeal."

Cody wasn't sure how to respond or even if he should.

"Good," the man said and made a let's-go gesture at the guy pushing his wheelchair.

The escort surrounding him blocked his view of everything that wasn't straight ahead but he saw enough to know it was definitely underground and it was mostly empty. Which didn't mean anything, he told himself. The country was lousy with underground parking garages, it was just a coincidence he'd seen that item on the news. LaDene had been right, he'd just been scaring himself. He wasn't a mobster, he was a courier, just a goddam courier. People didn't go around killing couriers. Nobody wanted that kind of trouble, the couriers' union was too well connected and too powerful.

A car engine started suddenly and the sound made him jump. The gray-haired man didn't even glance at him but the others moved in a little closer, hiding him from view. They stayed close, even after he heard the car pass, until they reached a bank of elevators. One was roped off with a sign that said it was out of service. The gray-haired man pressed the call button and twisted; it popped open on a hinge and he inserted a plain metal key.

The elevator doors opened and Cody caught a strong whiff of antiseptic mixed with something flowery. His stomach turned over as they rolled him into the car, facing the back so he couldn't see what floor they were going to. There was no voice announcement or even a chime but he could make out a series of faint, airy thumps—possibly just the motor running after a long period of disuse but Cody counted them anyway, noting when the air quality changed from rainforest to refrigerated, and estimated they stopped on the fourteenth or fifteenth floor.

The place looked like a fancy clinic, right down to the immaculate receptionist at the immaculate, shiny white desk. The gray-haired man gave her a brisk wave as he strode past, walking very quickly now as he led the way through a maze of corridors to a room with a gurney and the machine they were going to use on him.

"Take your robe off and get comfortable," the gray-haired man said, jerking a thumb at the gurney.

Cody obeyed, a bit surprised at how quickly everyone else had vanished, leaving him alone with the man. He held onto the robe, turning it sideways to use like a blanket. "You mind? I'm kinda cold."

"Already?" The man was doing something with the machine; he gave a small, humorless laugh. "Maybe we should get you some mitts and booties."

"You could turn down the air conditioning," Cody said.

No answer. Three people in white uniforms came in with a cart. Cody settled down with a sigh of resignation and closed his eyes so he wouldn't have to see the cannulas going in.

Setting up seemed to take forever, although as far as he could tell, the hardware was up to date and they were all competent enough. Whoever had put the cannulas in his arm and leg was genuinely talented; it had been almost painless. The blood-pressure cuff on his other arm was actually more uncomfortable. He didn't know why they needed that anyway, when the hospital gown would tell them whatever they needed to know about his vitals. But he supposed under the circumstances they wanted both a belt and suspenders. They even made a business of verifying his blood type and his DNA before they finally began the process of filtering his blood.

Once they got going, he felt a little lightheaded, as always, and colder than usual. He curled up as much as he could, huddling under the robe. There was very little conversation, all too low for him to make out; no one spoke to him. Eventually, he dozed off, mostly from boredom, and woke to find a pair of woolly socks on his feet. He didn't really feel any warmer but he was touched by the gesture all the same.

Just for something to do, he tried to guess who had done it, watching them surreptitiously as they moved around, checking read-outs from him, from the machine, from his blood. The black woman with shoulder-length braids looked like she could have been someone's mother; if so, it was someone very young. Parents of young children were usually good for a kind deed. Or it might have been the Chinese guy who, like Cody, seemed to be in his late thirties.

He couldn't decide about the older black woman. She checked his vitals more often than anyone else but that didn't necessarily mean she was more concerned about his welfare. For all he knew, the socks had come from old Gray Ponytail himself. Hadn't he mentioned something about booties before they'd even started? Or it was one of the other people he'd barely glimpsed, busily working with his blood somewhere behind him. Maybe between separating blood cells from plasma and pumping it back into him, someone had paused to think he might be cold.

It went on for hours. Cody dozed, woke, dozed again. His stomach growled and subsided as hunger pangs threatened to turn into queasiness. How much longer, he wondered, irritable with boredom and lack of food. If they didn't call a halt soon, he was going to have some kind of major blood sugar episode.

Almost as if he'd caught something of Cody's thoughts, the gray-haired man tapped him on the shoulder. "Are you supposed to eat something? Something in particular," he added, a bit impatiently.

"Food," Cody said, not caring how petulant he sounded.

"Not bread or sugar?"

"Just food. I don't suppose you'll give me any."

"What if we tried insulin instead?" There was an edge in the man's voice. In his peripheral vision, Cody saw the younger woman and the Chinese guy look up from a tablet they'd been studying together, obviously startled.

"Risky," Cody said. "I'm not diabetic. But you knew that."

The man gazed at him for some unmeasured period of time. He was worn out, tried and frustrated, Cody realized with a surge of spiteful joy; they all were but him most of all, because he was on the hook for whatever went wrong.

Abruptly, he blew out an exasperated breath and turned away. "We can't keep him any longer. Shut it down, give him lunch, and let's get him out of here."

Lunch turned out to be a can of nutrient with a straw; Cody was too hungry to feel more than a vague, momentary disappointment. The gray-haired man sat and glared at him. Hoping Cody would give up the goods somehow at the last minute? Or just being a sore loser?

"How old are you?" the man asked suddenly.

Cody paused and wiped his mouth. Considering how long they'd run his blood, he must have known, and a lot more besides. "Thirty-seven. Why?"

"Don't you think that's a little old to be a decoy?"

"I'm a courier." He went back to the drink.

"You're a decoy. A zero. A nothing. Less than nothing."

Cody had no response for that; he kept drinking.

"The one that sold you out, she was probably the *real* courier. Wasn't she?"

"Who?" But even as he asked, he knew. Her name was on the tip of his tongue but he managed not to say it aloud.

"I'm right, aren't I? You're just—what? A day-laborer who doesn't mind needles and won't faint at the sight of blood? *She's* carrying. LaVerne or LaRue, whatever her name is."

Cody pressed his lips together briefly. Whether the guy was telling the truth or fishing for a keyword, it wouldn't hurt not to give it to him. "Roughly ten percent of the population faints at the sight of blood," he said chattily. "It's a physical reaction, they can't help it. Nothing to do with their character or anything."

"Thank you for that piece of enlightenment." Despite his obvious irritation, his face was more impassive than ever, not to mention pastier. Now there were small flakes of what looked like dry skin around the man's hairline. The disguise was starting to break down, the wig parting company with the silicone mask. Everything probably should have been removed hours ago but the guy had kept nursing it along with touch-ups. Because he'd expected it would all by over by now, data extracted and delivered, payment collected and he'd be on his way to his next case, already forgetting what Cody looked like.

Instead he was sitting in a small, cold room with nothing to show for his effort but a spray-on about to peel off his face and nothing to look forward to except the displeasure of whoever he was working for, the loss of his fee, and a crew he had to pay anyway.

Cody finished the drink and set the empty can down beside him on the gurney. *Well*, that *wasn't fun. Whaddaya wanna do next?*

It was the last thought he had for a while.

Sounds nudged him gradually toward awareness, until he understood the voices and various other noises were real, not lingering fragments of dreams, or dream-like flashes from lost hours, possibly days. Eyes still closed, he rolled over, turning his face away from the bright light overhead and smelled clean sheets, along with alcohol, powder, and cleanser. Hospital emergency room, he thought with cautious relief; there were worse places to wake up.

His memory was patchy but he knew the basics of what had happened. As soon as his captors had been sure they wouldn't find anything in his blood, they no longer had to worry about contamination and dosed Cody's so-called lunch. Pretty heavily, if the lead-balloon sensation in his head was any indication. Just by way of kicking his ass for having nothing of value.

Once the lunch had taken effect, they had dressed him up and dumped him someplace where he could sleepwalk indefinitely without attracting attention. Like, say, a large mall. Or a shopping village; one with a multi-screen cineplex. Cody wondered how long he had been aimlessly roaming before anyone noticed something odd about him. There were all kinds of stories. Everybody in the union knew one about a courier who had woken up to find she'd wandered into a house and spent five days with people who'd thought she was a long-lost relative. Cody suspected that one was apocryphal.

Two days later, he was in a DC-area suburb, although he wasn't sure exactly which state. State-line ambiguity was getting to be a habit with him.

"How'd you like Oklahoma City?" asked the medic from where she sat at the lighting panel. She was a slightly plump woman with one brown eye and one blue eye; the difference was made more noticeable by the port wine stain covering that side of her face from hairline to the corner of her mouth.

"I only saw a parking garage, a clinic, and part of a hospital." Cody finished undressing and stood with his back to the plain white wall. "Ready when you are."

"Ah, you've done this before. I don't even have to tell you to close your eyes and hold perfectly still."

He took a breath and held it. Sometimes he imagined he could sense the UV light change as the scanning line traveled over his body. Years ago, when he had first become a courier, they'd showed him a video of himself being scanned. He'd thought he'd looked like a fantasy creature—one of Lewis Carroll's fabulous monsters that had wandered out of the looking glass into a high-tech lab.

Blaschko's Lines, a doctor had told him, years ago. Only visible under certain kinds of UV light.

He'd done research on his own, wondered about lesions or the possibility of waking up one morning to find himself permanently piebald. He would dream that the lines running up and down his arms and legs, traveling in waves on his torso, looping on his back, swirling all over his head would appear spontaneously and without warning in normal light; sometimes they were permanent. Other times, they'd flash on and off like a warning light.

He hadn't had that kind of anxiety dream in a long time. They'd faded away with the hotspots. Maybe now they were both coming back.

"Done," the medic called.

Relieved, Cody took a deep breath and stepped away from the wall to get dressed again. The medic asked his permission before she swabbed the inside of his cheek, and again before scraping a few skin cells from his lower back, his hip, and his knee. He was immensely grateful for the courtesy. It was always nice when someone treated a courier like a human being in a demanding profession rather than merely a meat-bag for data.

The guy who escorted him to his room for the night was was wearing the standard gopher attire—a multi-pocketed vest over plain t-shirt, jeans, and running shoes—but had a military bearing that he didn't even try to hide. Cody wasn't surprised to find someone waiting for him when he got there. It had been a while since the last sales pitch.

"We're all very glad to have you back safe." The woman in the swivel chair by the desk was dark-haired and dark-skinned and her voice had the faint but unmistakable lilt that Hindi speakers never lost completely. He had seen her before a few times, dressed as she was now in a black jacket and trousers, but only in passing. She was one of those people who gave the impression of being taller because of the way she carried herself. Not military-style like his friend now standing at obvious parade rest between himself and the door, just with authority. In charge. The touches of gray in her hair suggested she was older than he was, though he couldn't have said how much—more than ten, less than thirty.

"I'm glad to be back," he said, feeling a little awkward as he stood in front of her. She gestured for him to sit down on the bed, the only other furniture in the room, unless you counted the forty-inch screen in the wall.

"You automatically get a week of recuperation but we'll sign off on two or even three." She shrugged. "Or four."

"Thank you."

"This wasn't the first time for you, was it."

As if she didn't know, he thought, careful to keep a straight face. Then he realized she was actually waiting for an answer. "No," he said quickly. "It wasn't."

"I hope that it wasn't especially bad for you."

He shook his head. His memory was still quite spotty—his clearest recollection was of an older man with a ponytail and having to lie very still in a cold room while his blood was pumped out of his body and back in again. He also had the idea that there had been someone in the hotel room with him before he'd been kidnapped but that didn't seem likely. Considering how heavily he'd been drugged, he was probably lucky he still remembered his childhood.

Unless I rented it out for a database. Another of those left-field thoughts that had been popping into his head for the last few days. They'd probably meant something once.

" . . . sure you will be happy to know that your kidnappers came away with nothing," the woman was saying, "thanks to your unique . . . ah, condition."

He smiled a little. "I never thought of being a chimera as a condition like, oh, excessive perspiration. Or psoriasis."

"It does make you uniquely suited for deep encryption. Even if your kidnappers had thought to use your DNA to activate your blood, they wouldn't know you have more than one kind of DNA, much less that they needed to scan you under UV for the entire key."

His kidnappers; the way she said it made it sound almost as if they belonged to him in some way. Or like they were his personal problem—his *condition.*

"Eventually, that'll occur to someone. If someone else doesn't sell it to them first," he added. The memory of a woman's name, LaRue or LaDene, and an old movie flickered in his brain and was gone.

"Such optimism." She gave a short laugh. "The average merc can't afford to rent a full sequencer, let alone personnel to run it who would be smart enough to figure out you had two kinds of DNA, or that they'd need both for decryption." She gave another slightly heartier laugh. "Contrary to what you may have heard, the evil genius is mostly mythical. Nobody turns to crime because of their towering intellect.

"But that's neither here nor there. We still want you to work solely for us. I know that someone has made you this offer before—a few times, yes? As an employee, you would be paid substantially more, along with bonuses for crisis situations—"

"'Crisis situations?' Is that anything like 'hazardous duty'?"

She barely hesitated as she acknowledged his interruption. "Occupational benefits are also quite generous. Health coverage, vacation time, paternity leave—"

"Dental?"

Now she paused to give him a look. "And optical. Even a clothing allowance."

He was tempted to comment on how she had used hers but decided not to get personal.

"We can also be very flexible in terms of your cover," she went on. "Some sort of independent, low-key profession, like an accountant or a transcriber or—" she floundered suddenly and he could tell it wasn't something that happened to her very often.

"Software engineer," he suggested, then smiled sheepishly. "Kidding."

"That could work, as long as it's something nice and ordinary. Wedding albums, family albums, baby pictures, that sort of thing—"

"I really was kidding," he said. "Software mystifies me."

"You could even be semi-retired—"

"No." He shook his head, apologetic but firm. "If I go to work for you, I'm no longer a courier. I'm a government employee in a highly sensitive area under military jurisdiction. Once I lose my union membership, all bets are off. All I have is you."

"That's quite a lot," the woman said reprovingly. "You have no idea how much."

Actually, I do, he thought at her, *but if I'm flayed and hung up in a parking garage, I won't care about the cover story.* He shook his head again.

"If we take you into the fold, we can tell you more about what you're doing. Don't you want to know—"

"*No.*" It came out louder and more emphatic than he'd intended but he wasn't sorry. "I don't. You've got me this much. I agreed to cooperate because I don't need to be *in the fold* to be an encryption key. I'll keep the secret but I don't want to *be* the secret."

The woman shook her head. "Please. You went over that line a long time ago."

"Not quite," he insisted. "My body, yes. But not *me.*"

She stood up, stretching a little. "We'll talk again. This government doesn't give up that easily."

"Oh?" He raised his eyebrows. "Which government is that, anyway?"

The question caught her off-guard and for a moment she stared at him, open mouthed. Then she threw back her head and laughed. "Oh, very good," she said, as the man opened the door for her. "Very, *very* good." She started to leave, then hesitated. "And that's really your name: Cody."

"Yeah. My name's really Cody." Something flickered in his memory again but it was gone before he could think about it. He lay down on the bed and found the remote under one of the pillows.

"Well, *that* was fun," he said, to no one and to whatever bugs might be listening, and turned on the TV. "Now whaddaya wanna do?"

First published in *TRSF: The Best New Science Fiction,*
edited by Stephen Cass.

ABOUT THE AUTHOR

Pat Cadigan was born in Schenectady, New York, and now lives in London with her family. She made her first professional sale in 1980, and has subsequently come to be regarded as one of the best new writers of her generation. Her story "Pretty Boy Crossover" has appeared on several critic's lists as among the best science fiction stories of the 1980's, and her story "Angel" was a finalist for the Hugo Award, the Nebula Award, and the World Fantasy Award (one of the few stories ever to earn that rather unusual distinction). Her short fiction has been gathered in the collections *Patterns* and *Dirty Work*. Her first novel, *Mindplayers*, was released in 1987 and her second novel, *Synners*, released in 1991, won the Arthur C. Clarke Award as the year's best science-fiction novel, as did her third novel, *Fools*, making her the only writer ever to win the Clarke Award twice. She won the Hugo Award in 2013 for her story "The Girl-Thing Who Went Out For Sushi." Her other books include the novels *Dervish Is Digital, Tea from an Empty Cup,* and *Reality Used to Be a Friend of Mine, Cellular,* and, as editor, the anthology *The Ultimate Cyberpunk,* as well as two making-of movie books and four media tie-in novels. She is currently at work on a new novel set in the universe of "The Girl-Thing Who Went Out For Sushi."

The Vorkuta Event

KEN MACLEOD

1.
Tentacles and Tomes

It was in 19–, that unforgettable year, that I first believed that I had unearthed the secret cause of the guilt and shame that so evidently burdened Dr. David Rigley Walker, Emeritus Professor of Zoology at the University of G——. The occasion was casual enough. A module of the advanced class in Zoology dealt with the philosophical and historical aspects of the science. I had been assigned to write an essay on the history of our subject, with especial reference to the then not quite discredited notion of the inheritance of acquired characteristics. Most of my fellow students, of a more practical cast of mind than my own, were inclined to regard this as an irrelevant chore. Not I.

With the arrogance of youth, I believed that our subject, Zoology, had the potential to assimilate a much wider field of knowledge than its current practice and exposition was inclined to assume. Is not Man an animal? Is not, therefore, all that is human within, in principle, the scope of Zoology? Such, at least, was my reasoning at the time, and my excuse for a wide and—in mature retrospect—less than profitable reading. Certain recent notorious and lucrative popularizations—as well as serious studies of sexual and social behavior, pioneered by, of all people, entomologists—were in my view a mere glimpse of the empire of thought open to the zoologist. In those days such fields as evolutionary psychology, Darwinian medicine and ecological economics still struggled in the shattered and noisome eggshell of their intellectually and—more importantly—militarily crushed progenitors. The great reversal of the mid-century's verdict on this and other matters still slumbered in the womb of the future. These were, I may say, strange times, a moment of turbulent transition when the molecular doctrines were already established, but before they had become the very basis of biology. In the minds of older teachers and in the pages of obsolete textbooks certain questions now incontrovertible seemed novel and untried. The ghost of vitalism still walked the seminar room; plate tectonics was solid ground mainly to geologists; notions of intercontinental land bridges, and even fabled Lemuria, had not been altogether dispelled as worthy of at least serious dismissal. I deplored—nay, detested—all such vagaries.

So it was with a certain zeal, I confess, that I embarked on the background reading for my modest composition. I walked into the University library at noon, bounded up the stairs to the science floor, and alternated browsing the stacks and scribbling in my carrel for a good five hours. Unlike some of my colleagues, I had not afflicted myself with the nicotine vice, and was able to proceed uninterrupted save for a call of nature. I delved into Lamarck himself, in verbose Victorian translation; into successive editions of *The Origin of Species*; and into the *Journal of the History of Biology*. I had already encountered Koestler's *The Case of the Midwife Toad,* that devastating but regretful demolition of the Lamarckian claims of the fellow-traveling biologist, fraud, and suicide Viktor Kammerer—the book, in well-thumbed paperback, was an underground classic among zoology undergraduates, alongside Lyall Watson's *Supernature.* I read and wrote with a fury to discredit, for good and all, the long-exploded hypothesis that was the matter of my essay. But when I had completed the notes and outline, and the essay was as good as written, needing only some connecting phrases and a fair copy, a sense that the task was not quite finished nagged.

I leaned back in the plastic seat, and recollected of a sudden the very book I needed to deliver the *coup de grace.* But where had I seen it? I could almost smell it—and it was the sense of smell that brought back the memory of the volume's location. I stuffed my notes in a duffel bag, placed my stack of borrowings on the Returns trolley, and hurried from the library. Late in the autumn term, late in the day, the University's central building, facing me on the same hilltop as the tall and modern library, loomed black like a gothic mansion against the sunset sky. Against the same sky, bare trees stood like preparations of nerve-endings on an iodine-stained slide. I crossed the road and walked around the side of the edifice and down the slope to the Zoology Department, a granite and glass monument to the 1930s. Within: paved floors, tiled walls and hardwood balustrades, and the smell that had reminded me, a mingled pervasive waft of salt-water aquaria, of rat and rabbit droppings, of disinfectant and of beeswax polish. A porter smoked in his den, recognized me with a brief incurious glance. I nodded, turned and ascended the broad stone staircase. On the first landing a portrait of Darwin overhung the door to the top of the lecture hall; beneath the window lay a long glass case containing a dusty plastic model of *Architeuthys,* its two-meter tentacles outstretched to a painted prey. The scale of the model was not specified. At the top of the stairs, opposite the entrance to the library, stood another glass case, with the skeleton of a specimen of *Canis dirus* from Rancho La Brea. As I moved, the shadow and gleams of the dire wolf's teeth presented a lifelike snarl.

Inside, the departmental library was empty, its long windows catching the sun's last light. From the great table that occupied most of its space, the smell of beeswax rose like a hum, drowning out the air's less salubrious notes save that of the books that lined the walls. Here I had skimmed Schrödinger's neglected text on the nerves; here I had luxuriated in D'Arcy Thomson's glorious prose, the outpoured, ecstatic precision of *On Growth and Form*; here, more productively, I had bent until my eyes had watered over Mayr and Simpson and Dobzhansky. It was the last, I think, who had first sent me to glance, with a shudder, at the book I now sought.

There it was, black and thick as a Bible; its binding sturdy, its pages yellowing but sound, like a fine vellum. *The Situation in Biological Science: Proceedings of the Lenin Academy of Agricultural Sciences of the U.S.S.R., July 31—August 7, 1948, Complete Stenographic Report.* This verbatim account is one of the most sinister in the annals of science: it documents the conference at which the peasant charlatan Lysenko, who claimed that the genetic constitutions of organisms could be changed by environmental influences, defeated those of his opponents who still stood up for Mendelian genetics. Genetics in the Soviet Union took decades to recover.

I took the volume to the table, sat down and copied to my notebook Lysenko's infamous, gloating remark toward the close of the conference: "The Central Committee of the CPSU has examined my report and approved it'; and a selection from the rush of hasty recantations— announcements, mostly, of an overnight repudiation of a lifetime's study—that followed it and preceded the closing vote of thanks to Stalin. I felt pleased at having found—unfairly perhaps—something with which to sully further the heritage of Lamarck. At the same time I felt an urge to wash my hands. There was something incomprehensible about the book's very existence: was it naivety or arrogance that made its publishers betray so shameful a demonstration of the political control of science? The charlatan's empty victory was a thing that deserved to be done in the dark, not celebrated in a *complete stenographic report.*

But enough. As I stood to return the book to the shelf I opened it idly at the flyleaf, and noticed a queer thing. The sticker proclaiming it the property of the Department overlaid a handwritten inscription in broad black ink, the edges of which scrawl had escaped the bookplate's obliteration. I recognized some of the fugitive lettering as Cyrillic script. Curious, I held the book up to the light and tried to read through the page, but the paper was too thick.

The books were for reference only. The rule was strict. I was alone in the library. I put the book in my duffel bag and carried it to my bedsit. There, with an electric kettle on a shaky table, I steamed the bookplate off. Then, cribbing from a battered second-hand copy of *The Penguin Russian Course*, I deciphered the inscription. The Russian original has faded from my mind. The translation remains indelible:

To my dear friend Dr. Dav. R. Walker,
in memory of our common endeavor,
yours,
Ac. T. D. Lysenko.

The feeling that this induced in me may be imagined. I started and trembled as though something monstrous had reached out a clammy tentacle from the darkness of its lair and touched the back of my neck. If the book had been inscribed to any other academic elder I might have been less shocked: many of them flaunted their liberal views, and hinted at an earlier radicalism, on the rare occasions when politics were discussed; but Walker was a true-blue conservative of the deepest dye, as well as a mathematically rigorous Darwinian.

The next morning I trawled the second-hand bookshops of the University district. The city had a long, though now mercifully diminishing, "Red" tradition; and sure enough, I found crumbling pamphlets and tedious journals of that persuasion from the time of the Lysenko affair. In them I found articles defending Lysenko's views. The authors of some, the translators of others, variously appeared as: DRW, Dr. D. R. Walker, and (with a more proletarian swagger) Dave Walker. There was no room for doubt: my esteemed professor had been a Lysenkoist in his youth.

With a certain malice (forgivable in view of my shock and indeed dismay) I made a point of including these articles in my references when I typed up the essay and handed it in to my tutor, Dr. F——. A week passed before I received a summons to Professor Walker's office.

2.
Alcohol, Tobacco, and Ultraviolet Radiation Exposure

The Emeritus Professor was, as his title suggests, semi-retired; he took little part in the administration, and devoted his intermittent visits to the Department to the occasional sparkling but well-worn lecture; to shuffling and annotating off-prints of papers from his more productive days with a view to an eventual collection; and to some desultory research of his own into the anatomy and relationships of a Jurassic marine crocodile. Paleontology had been his field. In his day he had led expeditions to the Kalahari and the Gobi. He had served in the Second World War. In some biographical note I had glimpsed the rank of Lieutenant, but no reference to the Service in which it had been attained: a matter on which rumor had not been reticent.

The professor's office was at the end of one of the second story's long corridors. Dust, cobwebs, and a statistically significant sample of desiccated invertebrates begrimed the frosted glass panel of the door. I tapped, dislodging a dead spider and a couple of woodlice.

"Come in!"

As I stepped through the door the professor rose behind his desk and leaned forward. Tall and stooping, very thin, with weathered skin, sunken cheeks and a steely spade of beard, he seemed a ruin of his adventurous youth—more Quatermass than Quatermain, so to speak—but an impressive ruin. He shook hands across his desk, motioned me to a seat, and resumed his own. I brushed tobacco ash from friction-furred leather and sat down. The room reeked of pipe smoke and of an acetone whiff that might have been formaldehyde or whisky breath. Shelves lined the walls, stacked with books and petrified bones. Great drifts of journals and off-prints cluttered the floor. A window overlooking the building's drab courtyard sifted wan wintry light through a patina similar to that on the door. A fluorescent tube and an Anglepoise diminished even that effect of daylight.

Walker leaned back in his chair and flicked a Zippo over the bowl of his Peterson. He tapped a yellow forefinger-nail on a sheaf of paper, which I recognized without surprise as my essay.

"Well, Cameron," he said, through a gray-blue cloud, "you've done your homework."

"Thank you, sir," I said.

He jabbed the pipe-stem at me. "You're not at school," he said. "That is no way for one gentleman to address another."

"OK, Walker," I said, a little too lightly.

"Not," he went on, "that your little trick here was gentlemanly. You're expected to cite peer-reviewed articles, not dredge up political squibs and screeds from what you seized on as another chap's youthful folly. These idiocies are no secret. If you'd asked me, I'd have told you all about them—the circumstances, you understand. And I could have pointed you to the later peer-reviewed article in which I tore these idiocies, which I claimed as my own, to shreds. You could have cited that too. That would have been polite."

"I didn't intend any discourtesy," I said.

"You intended to embarrass me," he said. "Did you not?"

I found myself scratching the back of my head, embarrassed myself. My attempt at an excuse came out as an accusation.

"I found the inscription from Lysenko," I said.

Walker rocked back in his seat. "What?"

" 'To my dear friend Dr. David R. Walker, in memory of our common endeavor.' " Against my conscious will, the words came out in a jeering tone.

Walker planted his elbow-patches on his desk and cupped his chin in both hands, pipe jutting from his yellow teeth. He glared at me through a series of puffs.

"Ah, yes," he said at last. "That common endeavor. Would it perhaps pique your curiosity to know what it *was*?"

"I had assumed it was on genetics," I said.

"Hah!" snorted Walker. "You're a worse fool than I was, Cameron. What could I have done on genetics?"

"You wrote about it," I said, again sounding more accusing than I had meant to.

"I wrote rubbish for *The Modern Quarterly*," he said, "but I think you would be hard pressed to find in it anything about original work on genetics."

"I mean," I said, "your defense of him."

Walker narrowed his eyes. "These articles were written *after* I had received the book," he said. "So they were not what old Trofim was remembering me for, no indeed."

"So what was it?"

He straightened up. "A most disquieting experience," he said. "One that weighs on me even now. If I were to tell you of it, it would weigh on you for the rest of your life. And the strange thing is, Cameron, that I need not swear you to secrecy. The tale is as unbelievable as it is horrible. For you to tell it would merely destroy whatever credibility you have. Not only would nobody believe the tale—nobody would believe that I had told it to you. The more you insisted on it, the more you would brand yourself a liar and a fantasist of the first water."

"Then why should I believe it myself?"

His parchment skin and tombstone teeth grinned back his answer like a death's head illuminated from within.

"You will believe it."

I shrugged.

"You will wish you didn't," he added mildly. "You can walk out that door and forget about this, and I will forget your little jape. If you don't, if you stay here and listen to me, let me assure you that I will have inflicted upon you a most satisfactory revenge."

I squared to him from my seat. "Try me, Walker," I said.

3.
Walker's Account

Stalin's pipe was unlit—always a bad sign. Poskrebyshev, the General Secretary's sepulchral amanuensis, closed the door silently behind me. The only pool of light in the long, thickly curtained room was over Stalin's desk. Outside that pool two figures sat on high-backed chairs. A double glint on pince-nez was enough to warn me that one of these figures was Beria. The other, as I approached, I identified at once by his black flop of hair, his hollow cheeks, and his bright fanatic eyes: Trofim Lysenko. My knees felt like rubber. I had met Stalin before, of course, during the war, but I had never been summoned to his presence.

It was the summer of '47. I'd been kicking my heels in Moscow for weeks, trying without success—and more frustratingly, without definite refusal—to get permission to mount another expedition to the Gobi. It was not, of course, the best of times to be a British citizen in the Soviet capital. (It was not the best of times to be a Soviet citizen, come to that.) My wartime work in liaison may have been both a positive and a negative factor: positive, in that I had contacts, and a degree of respect; negative, in that it put me under suspicion—ludicrous though it may seem, Cameron—of being a spy. I might, like so many others, have gone straight from the Kremlin to the Lubianka.

Stalin rose, stalked towards me, shook hands brusquely, pointed me to a low seat—he was notoriously sensitive about his height—and returned to his desk chair. I observed him closely but covertly. He had lost weight. His skin was loose. He seemed more burdened than he had at Yalta and Tehran.

"Lieutenant Walker—" he began. Then he paused, favored me with a yellow-eyed, yellow-toothed smile, and corrected himself. "*Doctor* Walker. Rest assured, you were not invited here in your capacity as a British officer."

His sidelong glance at Beria told me all I needed to know about where I stood in that regard. Stalin sucked on his empty pipe, frowned, and fumbled a packet of Dunhills from his tunic. To my surprise, he proffered the pack across the desk. I took one, with fingers that barely trembled. A match flared between us; and for a moment, in that light, I saw that Stalin was afraid. He was more afraid than I; and that thought terrified me. I sank back and drew hard.

"We need your help, Dr. Walker. In a scientific capacity."

I hesitated, unsure how to address him. He was no comrade of mine, and to call him by his latest title, "Generalissimo," would have seemed fawning. My small diplomatic experience came to my aid.

"You surprise me, Marshal Stalin," I said. "My Soviet colleagues are more than capable."

Lysenko cleared his throat, but it was Beria who spoke. "Let us say there are problems."

"It is not," said Stalin, "a question of capability. It is important to us that the task we wish you to take part in be accomplished by a British scientist who is also a . . . former . . . British officer, who has—let us say—certain connections with certain services, and who is not—again, let us say—one who might, at some future date, be suspected of being connected with the organs of Soviet state security." Another sidelong glance at Beria.

"Let me be blunt, Marshal Stalin," I said. "You want me because I'm a scientist and because I you think I might be a British agent, and because you can be certain I'm not one of yours?"

"Fairly certain," said Stalin, with a dark chuckle.

Out of the corner of my eye I saw Beria flinch. I was startled that Stalin should hint so broadly of Soviet penetration of British intelligence, as well as of his mistrust of Beria. If I survived to return to England, I would make a point of reporting it directly to that chap who—Whitehall rumor had it—was in charge of stopping that sort of thing. What was his name again? Oh, yes—Philby. A moment later I realized that, very likely, Stalin and Beria had cooked up this apparent indiscretion between them, perhaps to test my reaction, or so that my very reporting of it might circuitously advance their sinister aims. But there were more pressing puzzles on my mind.

"But I'm a paleontologist!" I said. "What could there possibly be in that field that could be of interest to any intelligence service?"

"A good question," said Stalin. "An intriguing question, is it not? I see you are intrigued. All I can say at this point, Dr. Walker, is that you have only one way of finding the answer. If you choose not to help us, then I must say, with regret, that you must take the next flight for London. It may be impossible for you to return, or to dig again for the dinosaur bones of Outer Mongolia which appear to fascinate you so much. If you do choose to help us, not only will you find the answer to your question, but opportunities for further collaboration with our scientists might, one may imagine, open up."

The threat, mercifully small as it would have seemed to some, was dire to me; the offer tempting; but neither was necessary. I was indeed intrigued.

"I'll do it," I said.

"Good," said Stalin. "I now turn you over to the capable hands of ... "

He paused just long enough—a heartbeat—to scare me.

" ... Your esteemed colleague, Trofim Denisovich."

But, as though in amends for that small, cat-like moment of sporting with my fear, or perhaps from that sentimental streak which so often characterizes his type, his parting handshake was accompanied by momentary wetness of his yellow eyes and a confidential murmur, the oddest thing I ever heard—or heard of or read of—him say:

"God go with you."

Corridors, guards, stairs, the courtyard, more guards, then Red Square and the streets. Trofim walked fast beside me, hands jammed in his jacket pockets, his chin down; fifty-odd meters behind us, the pacing shadow of the man from the organs of state security. Beefy-faced women in kerchiefs mixed concrete by shovel, struggled with wheel-barrows, took bawled orders from loutish foremen. Above them, on the bare scaffolding of the building sites, huge red-bordered black-on-white banners flapped, vast magnifications of a flattering ink portrait of the face I had seen minutes before. There seemed to be no connection, the merest passing resemblance to the aged, pock-marked man. I recalled something he had, it was told, once snarled at his drunken, vainglorious son, who'd pleaded, "After all, I too am Stalin." He'd said:

"*You* are not Stalin! *I* am not Stalin! Stalin is a banner ... "

At that moment I thought I could quite literally see what he'd meant.

"Well, David Rigley," said Lysenko (evidently under the misapprehension that my second name was a patronymic), "the leading comrades have landed you and me in a fine mess."

"You know what this is about?"

"I do, more's the pity. We may be doomed men. Let us walk a little. It's the safest way to talk."

"But surely—"

"Nothing is 'surely,' here. You must know that. Even a direct order from the Boss may not be enough to protect us from the organs. Beria is building atomic bombs out on the tundra. Where he gets his labor force from, you can guess. Including engineers and scientists, alas. At one of their sites they have found something that . . . they want us to look into."

"Atomic bombs? With respect, Trofim Denisovich—"

"I will not argue with you on that. But what Beria's . . . men have found is more terrifying than an atomic bomb. That is what we have agreed to investigate, you and I."

"Oh," I said. "So that's what I've agreed to. Thanks for clearing that up." The sarcasm was wasted on him.

"You are welcome, David Rigley." He stopped at an intersection. A black car drew up beside us. He waved me to the side door. I hung back.

"It is my own car," he said mildly. "It will take us to my farm. Tomorrow, it will take us to the airport."

Lysenko's private collective farm—so to speak—in the Gorki-Leninskie hills south of Moscow was of course a showcase, and was certainly a testimony more to Lysenko's enthusiasm than to his rigor, but I must admit that it was a hospitable place, and that I spent a pleasant enough afternoon there being shown its remarkable experiments, and a very pleasant evening eating some of the results. For that night, Trofim and I could pretend to have not a care in the world—and in that pretence alone, I was of one mind with the charlatan.

The following morning we flew to the east and north. It was not a civilian flight. Aeroflot's reputation is deservedly bad enough; but it is in the armed forces that Aeroflot pilots learn their trade. This flight in an LI-2 transport was courtesy of the Army. Even now, the memory of that flight brings me out in a cold sweat. So you will forgive me if I pass over it. Suffice it to say that we touched down on a remote military airfield that evening to refuel and to change pilots, and continued through a night during which I think I slept in my cramped bucket seat from sheer despair. We landed—by sideslip and steep, tight spiral, as if under fire—just after dawn the following morning on a bumpy, unpaved strip in the midst of a flat, green plain. A shack served as a terminal building, before which a welcoming committee of a dozen or so uniformed men stood. Through a small porthole, as the plane juddered to a halt, I glimpsed some more distant structures: a tower on stilts, long low barracks, a mine-head, and great heaps of spoil. There may have been a railway line. I'm not sure.

Trofim and I unkinked our backs, rubbed grit from our eyes, and made our stooping way to the hatch. I jumped the meter drop to the ground. Trofim sat and swung his long legs over and slid off more carefully. The air was fine and fresh, unbelievably so after Moscow, and quite warm. One of the men detached himself from the line-up and hurried over. He was stocky, blue-jowled, with a look of forced joviality on his chubby, deep-lined face. He wore a cap with the deep blue band of the security organs. Shaking hands, he introduced himself as Colonel Viktor A. Marchenko. He led us to the shack, where he gave us glasses of tea and chunks of sour black bread, accompanied by small talk and no information, while his men remained at attention outside—they didn't smoke or shuffle—then took us around the back of the shack to a Studebaker flat-bed truck. To my surprise, the colonel took the driver's seat. Trofim and I squeezed in beside him. The rest of the unit piled perilously on the back.

We associate Russia's far north with snow and ice. Its brief summer is almost pleasant, apart from the mosquitoes and the landslides. Small flowers carpet the tundra. Its flat appearance is deceptive, concealing from a distance the many hollows and rises of the landscape. The truck went up and down, its tires chewing the unstable soil. At the crest of each successive rise the distant buildings loomed closer. The early-morning sun glinted on long horizontal lines in front of them: barbed wire, no doubt, and not yet rusty. It became obvious, as I had of course suspected, that this was a labor camp. I looked at Lysenko. He stared straight ahead, sweat beading his face. I braced my legs in the foot-well and gripped my knees hard.

At the top of a rise the truck halted. The colonel nodded forward, and made a helpless gesture with his hand. Trofim and I stared in shock at what lay in front of us. At the bottom of the declivity, just a few meters down the grassy slope from the nose of the truck, the ground seemed to have given way. The hole was about fifteen meters across and four deep. Scores of brown corpses, contorted and skeletal, protruded at all angles from the ragged black earth. From the bottom of the hole, an edged metallic point stood up like the tip of a pyramid or the corner of an enormous box. Not a speck of dirt marred the reflective sheen of its blue-tinted, silvery surfaces.

My first thought was that some experimental device, perhaps one of Beria's atomic bombs, had crashed here among some of the camp's occupants, killing and half-burying the poor fellows. My second thought was that it had exposed the mass grave of an earlier batch of similar unfortunates. I kept these thoughts to myself and stepped down from the cab, followed by Lysenko. The colonel jumped out the other side and barked an order. Within seconds his men had formed a widely spaced cordon around the hole, each standing well back, with his Kalashnikov leveled.

"Take a walk around it," said Marchenko.

We did, keeping a few steps away from the raw edge of the circular gash. About three meters of each edge of the object was exposed. Lysenko stopped and walked to the brink. I followed, to peer at a corpse just below our feet. Head, torso and one outflung arm poked out of the soil. Leathery skin, a tuft of hair, empty sockets and a lipless grin.

"From the . . . *Yezhovschina?*" I asked, alluding to the massacres of a decade earlier.

Trofim leaned forward and pointed down. "I doubt," he said dryly, "that any such died with bronze swords in their hands."

I squatted and examined the body more closely. Almost hidden by a fall of dirt was the other hand, clutching a hilt that did indeed, between the threads of a rotten tassel, have a brassy gleam. I looked again at what shock had made me overlook on the others: stubs of blades, scraps of gear, leather belts and studs, here and there around withered necks a torc of a dull metal that might have been pewter.

"So who are they?" I asked.

Lysenko shrugged.

"Tartars, Mongols . . . "

His knowledge of history was more dubious than his biology. These peoples had never migrated so far north, and no Bronze Age people was native to the area. The identity and origin of the dead barbarians puzzles me to this day.

Around the other side of the pit, the side that faced the camp, things were very different. The upper two meters of that face of the pyramid was missing, as if it was the opened top of that hypothetical box's corner. And the bodies—I counted ten—scattered before it were definitely those of camp laborers: thin men in thin clothes, among flung shovels. The corpses looked quite fresh. Only their terrible rictus faces were like those of the other and more ancient dead.

"What is this?" I asked Lysenko. "One of Beria's infernal machines?"

He shot me an amused, impatient glance.

"You overestimate us," he said. "This is not a product of our technology. Nor, I venture to suggest, is it one of yours."

"Then whose?"

"If it is not from some lost civilization of deep antiquity, then it is not of this world."

We gazed for a while at the black empty triangle and then completed our circuit of the pit and returned to Marchenko, who still stood in front of the truck.

"What happened here?" Lysenko asked.

Marchenko pointed towards the camp, then down at the ground.

"This is a mining camp," he said. "The mine's galleries extend beneath our feet. Some days ago, there was a cave-in. It resulted in a rapid subsidence on the surface, and exposed the object, and the slain warriors. A small squad of prisoners was sent into the pit to investigate, and to dig out the bodies and artifacts. To be quite frank, I suspect that they were sent to dig for valuables, gold and what not. One of them, for reasons we can only speculate, tried to enter the aperture in the object. Within moments, they were all dead."

"Tell us plainly," said Lysenko. "Do you mean they were shot by the guards?"

The colonel shook his head. "They could have been," he said, "for disobeying orders. But as it happens, they were not. Something from the object killed them without leaving a mark. Perhaps a poisonous gas—I don't know. That is for you to find out."

His story struck as improbable, or at least incomplete, but this was no time to dispute it.

"For heaven's sake, man!" I cried out. "And get killed ourselves?"

Marchenko bared a gold incisor.

"That is the problem, yes? You are scientists. Solve it."

This insouciance for a moment infuriated us, but solve it we did. An hour or two later, after the truck had returned from the camp with the simple equipment we'd demanded, Lysenko and I were standing in the pit a couple of meters from the black aperture. Behind us the truck chugged, its engine powering a searchlight aimed at the dark triangle. Trofim guided a long pole, on the end of which one of the truck's wing mirrors was lashed. I stood in front of him, the pole resting on my shoulder, and peered at the mirror with a pair of binoculars requisitioned from (no doubt) a camp guard. Nothing happened as our crude apparatus inched above the dark threshold. We moved about, Trofim turning the mirror this way and that. The magnified mirror image filled a large part of the close-focus view.

"What do you see?" Lysenko asked.

"Nothing," I said. "Well, the joins of the edges. They go as far as I can see. Below it there's just darkness. It's very deep."

We backed out and scrambled up.

"How big is this thing?" I asked Marchenko.

He shifted and looked sideways, then jabbed a finger downward.

"A similar apex," he said, "pokes down into the gallery beneath us."

"How far beneath us?"

His tongue flicked between his lips for a moment.

"About a hundred meters"

"If this is a cube," I said, "four hundred feet diagonally—my God!"

"We have reason to think it is a cube," said Marchenko.

"Take us to the lower apex," said Lysenko.

"Do you agree?" Marchenko asked me.

"Yes," I said.

A sign arched over the camp entrance read:

"Work in the USSR is a matter of honor and glory." For all that we could see as the truck drove in, nobody in the camp sought honor and glory that day. Guards stood outside every barracks door. Three scrawny men were summoned to work the hoist. Marchenko's squad took up positions around the mine-head. Lysenko, Marchenko and I—with one of Marchenko's sergeants carrying the pole and mirror—descended the shaft in a lift cage to the gallery. Pitchblende glittered in the beams from our helmet lamps. We walked forward for what seemed like many hours, but according to my watch was only fifty-five minutes. The cave-in had been cleared. Down like the point of a dagger came the lower apex of the cube, its tip a few inches above the floor. Its open face was not black but bright. It cast a blue light along the cavern.

"Well," said Lysenko, with a forced laugh, "this looks more promising."

This time it was I who advanced with the pole and angled the mirror in; Lysenko who looked through the Zeiss. I saw a reflected flash, as though something had moved inside the object. Blue light, strangely delimited, strangely slow, like some luminous fluid, licked along the wooden pole. With a half-second's warning, I could have dropped it. But as that gelid lightning flowed over my hands, my fingers clamped to the wood. I felt a forward tug. I could not let go. My whole body spasmed as if in electric shock, and just as painfully. My feet rose off the ground, and my legs kicked out behind me. At the same moment I found myself flying forward like a witch clinging to a wayward broom. With a sudden flexure that almost cracked my spine, I was jerked through the inverted triangular aperture and upward into the blue-lit space above. That space was not empty. Great blocks of blue, distinct but curiously insubstantial, floated about me. I was borne upwards, then brought to a halt. I could see, far above, a small triangle of daylight, in equally vivid contrast to the darkness immediately beneath it and the unnatural light around me. Apart from my hands, still clutched around the pole, my muscles returned to voluntary control. I hung there, staring, mouth open, writhing like a fish on a hook. My throat felt raw, my gasps sounded ragged. I realized that I had been screaming. The echoes of my screams rang for a second or two in the vast cubical space.

Before my eyes, some of the blocky shapes took on a new arrangement: a cubist caricature of a human face, in every detail down to the teeth. Eyes like cogwheels, ears like coffins. From somewhere came an impression, nay, a conviction, that this representation was meant to be *reassuring*. It was not.

What happened next is as difficult to describe as a half-remembered dream: a sound of pictures, a taste of words. I had a vision of freezing space, of burning suns, of infinite blackness shot through with stars that were not eternal: stars that I might outlive. I heard the clash of an enormous conflict, remote in origin, endless in prospect, and pointless in issue. It was not a war of ideals, but an ideal war: what Plato might have called the Form of War. Our wars of interests and ideologies can give only the faintest foretaste of it. But a foretaste they are. I was given to understand—how, I do not know—that joining in such a war is what the future holds for our descendants, and for all intelligent species. It is conducted by machines that carry in themselves the memories, and are themselves the only monuments, of the races that built them and that they have subsumed. This is a war with infinite casualties, infinite woundings, and no death that is not followed—after no matter what lapse of time—by a resurrection and a further plunge into that unending welter. No death save that of the universe itself can release the combatants, and only at that terminus will it have meaning, and then only for a moment, the infinitesimal moment of contemplating a victory that is final because it precedes, by that infinitesimal moment, the end of all things: victory pure and undefiled, victory for its own sake, the victory of the last mind left.

This hellish vision was held out to me as an inducement! Yes, Cameron—I was being offered the rare and unthinkable privilege of joining the ranks of warriors in this conflict that even now shakes the universe; of joining it centuries or millennia before the human race rises to that challenge itself. I would join it as a mind: my brain patterns copied and transmitted across space to some fearsome new embodiment, my present body discarded as a husk. And if I refused, I would be cast aside with contempt. The picture that came before me—whether from my own mind, or from that of the bizarre visage before me—was of the scattered bodies in the pit.

With every fiber of my being, and regardless of consequence, I screamed my refusal. Death itself was infinitely preferable to that infinite conflict.

I was pulled upward so violently that my arms almost dislocated. The blue light faded, blackness enveloped me, and then the bright triangle loomed. I hurtled through it and fell with great force, face down in the mud. The wind was knocked out of me. I gasped, choked, and lifted my head painfully up, to find myself staring into the sightless eyes of one of the recent dead, the camp laborers. I screamed again, scrambled to my feet, and clawed my way up the crumbling side of the pit. For a minute I stood quite alone.

Then another body hurtled from the aperture, and behaved exactly as I had done, including the scream. But Lysenko had my outstretched hand to grasp his wrist as he struggled up.

"Were you pulled in after me?" I asked.

Lysenko shook his head.

"I rushed to try to pull you back."

"You're a brave man," I said.

He shrugged.

"Not brave enough for what I found in there."

"You saw it?" I asked.

"Yes," he said. He shuddered. "Before that Valhalla, I would choose the hell of the priests."

"What we saw," I said, "is entirely compatible with materialism. That's what's so terrifying."

Lysenko clutched at my lapels. "No, not materialism! Mechanism! Man must fight that!"

"Fight it . . . endlessly?"

His lips narrowed. He turned away.

"Marchenko lied to us," he said.

"What?"

Lysenko nodded downward at the nearest bodies. "That tale of his—these men were not sent into this pit here, and killed by something lashing out from the . . . device. These men are *miners*. They entered it exactly as we did, from below."

"So why are they dead, and we're alive?" As soon as I asked the question, I knew the answer. Only their bodies were dead. Their minds were on their way to becoming alive somewhere else.

"You remember the choice you were given," said Lysenko. "They chose differently."

"They chose *that*—over—?" I jerked a backward thumb.

"Yes," said Lysenko. "A different hell."

We waited. After a while the truck returned from the camp.

4.
Fallout Patterns

Walker fell silent in the lengthened shadows and thickened smoke.

"And then what happened?" I asked.

He knocked out his pipe. "Nothing," he said. "Truck, plane, Moscow, Aeroflot, London. My feet barely touched the ground. I never went back."

"I mean, what happened to the thing you found?"

"A year or two later, the site was used for an atomic test."

"Over a uranium mine?"

"I believe that was part of the object. To maximize fallout. That particular region is still off limits, I understand."

"How do you know this?"

"You should know better than to ask," said Walker.

"So Stalin had your number!"

He frowned. "What do you mean?"

"He guessed correctly," I said. "About your connections."

"Oh yes. But leave it at that." He waved a hand, and began to refill his pipe. "It's not important."

"Why did he send a possible enemy agent, and a charlatan like Lysenko? Why not one of his atomic scientists, like Sakharov?"

"Sakharov and his colleagues were otherwise engaged," Walker said. "As for sending me and Lysenko . . . I've often wondered about that myself. I suspect he sent me because he wanted the British to know. Perhaps he wanted us worried about worse threats than any that might come from him, and at the same time worried that his scientists could exploit the strange device. Lysenko—well, he was reliable, in his way, and expendable, unlike the real scientists."

"Why did you write what you did, about Lysenko?"

"One." Walker used his pipe as a gavel on the desk. "I felt some gratitude to him. Two." He tapped again. "I appreciated the damage he was doing."

"To Soviet science?"

"Yes, and to science generally." He grinned. "I was what they would call an enemy of progress. I still am. Progress is progress towards the future I saw in that thing. Let it be delayed as long as possible."

"But you've contributed so much!"

Walker glanced around at his laden shelves. "To paleontology. A delightfully useless science. But you may be right. Even the struggle against progress is futile. Natural selection eliminates it. It eliminated Lysenkoism, and it will eliminate my efforts. The process is ineluctable. Don't you see, Cameron? It is not the failure of progress, the setbacks, that are to be feared. It is progress itself. The most efficient system will win in the end. The most advanced machines. And the machines, when they come into their own, will face the struggle against the other machines that are already out there in the universe. And in that struggle, anything that does not contribute to the struggle—all beauty, all knowledge, all scruple—will be discarded or eliminated. There will be nothing left but the bare will, the will to win, and the means to that end." He sighed. "In his own mad way, Lysenko understood that. There was a sort of quixotic nobility in his struggle against the logic of evolution, in his belief that man could humanize nature. No. Man is a brief interlude between the prehuman and the posthuman. To protract that interlude is the most we can hope for."

He said nothing more, except to tell me that he had recommended my essay for an A++.

The gesture was kind, considering how I had provoked him, but it did me little good. I failed that year's examinations. In the summer I worked as a laborer in a nearby botanic garden, and studied hard in the evenings. In this way I made up for lost time in the areas of zoology in which I had been negligent, and re-sat the examination with success. But I maintained my interest in those theoretical areas which I'd always found most fascinating, and specialized in my final year in evolutionary genetics, to eventually graduate with First Class Honors.

I told no one of Walker's story. I did not believe it at the time, and I do not believe it now. Since the fall of the Soviet Union, many new facts have been revealed. No nuclear test ever took place at Vorkuta. There was no uranium mine at the place whose location can be deduced from Walker's account. There is no evidence that Lysenko made any unexplained trips, however brief, to the region. No rumors about a mysterious object found near a labor camp circulate even in that rumor-ridden land. As for Walker himself, his Lysenkoism was indeed about as genuine ("let us say," as Stalin might have put it) as his Marxism. There is evidence, from other and even more obscure articles of his, and from certain published and unpublished memoirs and reminiscences that I have come across over the years, that he was a Communist between 1948 and 1956. Just how this is connected with his inclusion in the

New Year Honors List for 1983 ("For services to knowledge") I leave for others to speculate. The man is dead.

I owe to him, however, the interest which I developed in the relationship between, if you like, Darwinian and Lamarckian forms of inheritance. This exists, of course, not in biology but in artificial constructions. More particularly, the possibility of combining genetic algorithms with learned behavior in neural networks suggested to me some immensely fertile possibilities. Rather to the surprise of my colleagues, I chose for my postgraduate research the then newly established field of computer science. There I found my niche, and eventually obtained a lectureship at the University of E———, in the Department of Artificial Intelligence.

The work is slow, with many setbacks and false starts, but we're making progress.

First published in *The New and Perfect Man (Postscripts #24/25)*, edited by Peter Crowther and Nick Gevers.

ABOUT THE AUTHOR

Ken MacLeod graduated with a B.Sc. in Zoology from Glasgow University in 1976. Following research in bio-mechanics at Brunel University, he worked as a computer analyst/programmer in Edinburgh. He's now a full-time writer, and widely considered to be one of the most exciting new SF writers to emerge in the '90s, his work featuring an emphasis on politics and economics rare in the New Space Opera, while still maintaining all the widescreen, high-bit-rate, action-packed qualities typical of the form. His first two novels, *The Star Fraction* and *The Stone Canal,* each won the Prometheus Award. His other books include the novels, *The Sky Road, The Cassini Division, Cosmonaut Keep, Dark Light, Engine City, Newton's Wake, Learning the World, The Restoration Game,* and *Intrusion,* plus a novella chapbook, *The Human Front,* and a collection, *Strange Lizards from Another Galaxy.* His most recent book is a new novel, *Descent.* He lives in West Lothian, Scotland, with his wife and children.

"We're All Dreaming," Arctor Said: Drugs in Science Fiction, from the 1960s to the Present

ALVARO ZINOS-AMARO

Open any of the best-known science fiction books from about 1965 to 1975 and the odds are that you'll find some reference to drugs. This isn't surprising. The 1960s, after all, were rife with upheavals. Escalating involvement in the Vietnam War, the threat of nuclear apocalypse with the 1962 Cuban missile crisis, the assassination of President John F. Kennedy in 1963, the moon landing of 1969, and the civil rights, youth and counterculture movements—just to name a few—represent some of the decade's many instances of social and political dislocation.

In the counterculture, the use of drugs such as marijuana, LSD, peyote, psilocybin mushrooms and other psychedelics blossomed. Partially as a result of the same restless impulse to experiment, to seek new forms of awareness and self-expression, that fueled the counterculture, science fiction's popularity grew.

This interest attracted new writers, many of them well versed in contemporary literature and theory, into the field. Science fiction entered a transformative phase known as the New Wave. During the New Wave, genre writers relied primarily on modernist prose techniques to explore subjects like sex, overpopulation, non-Western religions, ecology, environmentalism, entropy, and "inner space," often trying to break taboos along the way.

As a literature that extrapolates technological change but also tends to reflect the times in which it's written, it was perhaps inevitable that much New Wave science fiction would feature drugs.

Consider a few examples. Perhaps the most powerful plot device in Frank Herbert's *Dune* (1965) is the spice "melange," literally the most valuable commodity in the universe[1]. Herbert's subsequent *The Santaroga Barrier* (1968) posits an alternate society built around the consumption of the fictional psychedelic "Jaspers."

Brian Aldiss' *Barefoot in the Head* (1969) uses Joycean language to chronicle the new, permanently tripped out society that arises from the ashes of the old as a result of an "acid-head war." Philip K. Dick's[2] *The Three Stigmata of Palmer Eldritch* (1965) and *Now Wait for Last Year* (1966) deal with various layers of reality and disembodied consciousnesses moving through time. Early stories by Norman Spinrad, such as "Carcinoma Angels" (1967), "No Direction Home" (1972) and "The Weed of Time" (1973), as well as novels like *The Men in the Jungle* (1967) and *Bug Jack Barron* (1969), all entail drug use.

In Robert Silverberg's *Downward to the Earth* (1970) the protagonist is able to achieve ecstatic communion with the alien planet's elephant-like beings via hallucinogens; and in Silverberg's *A Time of Changes* (1971) a culture which proscribes the sharing of the self is confronted with a telepathy-facilitating drug.

In John Brunner's *The Stone That Never Came Down* (1973), the drug "VC" (viral coefficient) boosts intelligence and memory, leading to an overall saner world[3]. The notion of a dystopia in which drugs are used by the state to control the population, an old idea[4], was explored in George Lucas' film *THX 1138* (1971).

And in the grim future of Stanley Kubrick's *A Clockwork Orange* (1971), which adapted a novella by Anthony Burgess, "Milkbars" dispensed the drug-laced "milk-plus."

During this period, then, the relationship between drugs in society and drugs in SF appears relatively straightforward: their explosion in the former was recorded in the latter.

But what has happened between 1973 and today?

After the Wave Crashed

During the 1970s, drug use in the US (expressed as a percentage of its population) reached a peak. By 1979, 14.1% of those aged twelve or older were reporting illicit consumption of marijuana, cocaine, hallucinogens, inhalants, heroin, or nonmedical use of sedatives, tranquilizers, stimulants, or analgesics during the last month[5]. Despite the fact that President Nixon began a "war on drugs" in 1971, public perception of drugs as a societal problem was low throughout the decade.

The Gallup poll, which asks a population sample, "What do you think is the most important problem facing this country today?", reported that only 20% of those asked named drugs as part of their answer in 1973, and by late 1979, there was barely mention of drugs in survey responses[6]. So while drug usage was elevated, drugs were no longer a topic of intense social discourse.

In broad terms, 1970s science fiction reflects this. The New Wave came to an end, but its crash left many writers' and readers' expectations reconfigured. Andrew Butler uses the term "amphicatastrophe" to describe 1970s narratives: they avoid the happy, often redemptive endings typical of what J. R. R. Tolkien dubbed "eucatastrophes," but also the catharsis that derives from the protagonists' failure in what Tolkien named "dyscatastrophes."[7]

1970s science fiction consistently questions assumptions about heterosexuality, patriarchy and capitalism, and other "invisible enemies"[8]. Drugs may enable these conversations, but aren't necessarily part of the discussions themselves, as in, for example, Thomas M. Disch's *334* (1972), Ian Watson's *The Embedding* (1973) or Joanna Russ' *We Who Are About To . . .* (1977).

This does not mean that all, or even, most key texts of the 1970s trade in drugs, even as a conduit to other issues. In fact, many artists and readers went flocking in the opposite direction, seeking the more familiar comforts of adventure-driven fiction: the decade saw a swell of sword-and-planetary romances, Tolkien imitators and fantasy role-playing games, as well as big-budget films and series like *Star Wars* (1977), *Superman* (1978), *Battlestar Galactica* (1978-1979) and *Flash Gordon* (1980). These works don't reflect any sense of crisis or preoccupation with drugs[9].

Somewhere between those trying to break the mold and those seeking solace within its confines, were veteran writers like Isaac Asimov, Robert A. Heinlein, Arthur C. Clarke, Clifford D. Simak and Leigh Brackett. Their 1970s output is often not in direct dialogue with contemporary trends, and is best understood in the context of those writers' individual and idiosyncratic careers.

"Say Hello to My Little Friend!"

In the 1980s, illicit drug consumption decreased, falling from the previously stated 14.1% to 12.1% by 1985[10]. However, the perception of drug abuse as a major societal ill began to increase, from 2-3% in the mid 1980s up to 64% in 1989[11]. If drug usage decreased significantly (down to 7.7% by 1988, just one year before that survey), why did public awareness of it skyrocket?

The answer is the cocaine/crack cocaine "epidemic" of the 1980s[12]. The phenomenon received intense media coverage, and imprinted itself strongly on the national consciousness. Non-genre films like *Scarface* (1983), *Less than Zero* (1987), *Clean and Sober* (1988), *Bright Lights, Big City* (1988) and even B-grade action vehicles like *Death Wish 4: The Crackdown* (1987) and *Delta Force 2: The Colombian Connection* (1990) portrayed the epidemic on all scales, from the personal to the international.

Within science fiction films, cocaine itself is less evident. Ken Russell's *Altered States* (1980), with its psychedelics, was in sense a throwback to the New Wave; David Cronenberg's *Scanners* (1981) featured "ephemerol," a drug that both created telepaths and was able to dampen their abilities; Gerald Potterton's *Heavy Metal* (1981) offered viewers "plutonian nyborg," which looked like cocaine but produced marijuana-like effects; David Lynch's adaptation of *Dune* (1984) brought melange to the big screen; Mark L. Lester's film version of Stephen King's *Firestarter* (1984) linked the hallucinogen "LOT-6" with telepathy and pyrokinesis; Graham Baker's *Alien Nation* (1988) introduced "Jabroka," which could control the film's alien Newcomers without harming humans.

Perhaps only Irvin Kershner's *RoboCop 2* (1990) featured a stand-in for crack cocaine, in the form of the highly addictive, aggression-causing narcotic "Nuke."

Histories of written science fiction typically identify the 1980s with cyberpunk, which regularly featured drug use. Reflecting this, Kim Stanley Robinson once provided a "recipe" for cyberpunk, and one of the ingredients was "a half gram of Dexadrine."[13]

The novel most often identified with cyberpunk is William Gibson's *Neuromancer* (1984), whose main characters all use "Pills," "Derms," or other needle-injected substances. John Shirley's *Eclipse* or A Song Called Youth trilogy (1985-1990) depicts the trade and use of "sink," or synthetic cocaine, as well as other more baroque forms of intoxication.

Later cyberpunk descendants, like Neal Stephenson's *Snow Crash* (1992), whose "snow crash" doubles as both computer virus and central nervous system viral disease, were more explicitly innovative as relates to drugs, by blending the technological with the biological.

We should also remember that while cyberpunk was an important movement during this decade, drugs continued to appear in non-cyberpunk science fiction as well. The acclaimed early short stories from this period by Lucius Shepard, for instance, regularly depict characters in the throes of drug addiction[14].

And of course, as in the 1970s, many writers were working in non-cyberpunk modes that didn't make much use of drugs: Gregory Benford's *Timescape* (1980), Joan D. Vinge's *The Snow Queen* (1980), Orson Scott Card's *Ender's Game* (1985), Brian Aldiss' Helliconia Trilogy (1982-1985) and Dan Simmons' *Hyperion* (1989) are a few examples.

Strange Days Indeed

In the 1990s illicit drug usage continued to decline, averaging about 6.2%. Cocaine use saw a stark reduction from 1980s levels. Reported lifetime heroin use, however, began to increase: in 1990 it was 0.8%, and, despite fluctuations, by 1999 it had reached 1.4%. During this decade, use of ecstasy (MDMA), often linked with the rave and club scenes, also increased.

The history of science fiction during the 1990s is complex, and has been less critically examined than previous decades. At least three different trends have been identified, though: a resurgence of space opera (technological globalization in part replacing cyberpunk's imagined global slum), a preponderance of apocalyptic and singularity-oriented narratives, and increased porosity in perceived genre boundaries[15].

We begin to see, then, a considerable fragmentation of an already-divided genre. Drugs are still a crucial element of some of the decade's important books: the "feathers" in Jeff Noon's *Vurt* (1993), for example, were not only hallucinogens, but provided a gateway to a shared alternate reality, while the immunosuppressant drugs (and cosmetic surgeries) routinely administered to the natives of a colony planet in Paul Park's *Coelestis* (1993) allowed these aliens to be remolded into human shape.

But many of the decade's significant works—such as Greg Bear's *Queens of Angels* (1990), John Varley's *Steel Beach* (1992), Kim Stanley Robinson's Mars trilogy (1993-1996), Vernor Vinge's *A Fire Upon the Deep* (1992), Connie Willis' *Doomsday Book* (1992), Nancy Kress' *Beggars in Spain* (1993) and Octavia Butler's *Parable of the Sower* (1993) and *Parable of the Talents* (1998)—make little more than occasional drug references.

The science fiction television landscape, however, tells another story: perhaps by now it was starting to catch up with the drug tropes that had been explored on the page in previous decades. *Alien Nation*'s (1989-1990) "digitalin," *TekWar*'s (1994-1996) eponymous "tek," *Babylon 5*'s (1993-1998) "dust," "Sleepers" and "stims," and *Star Trek: Deep Space*

Nine's (1993-1999) "Ketracel-white" were all vital parts of these shows' ongoing stories, rather than the subject of one-off episodes. In film, Brett Leonard's *The Lawnmower Man* (1992) treated VR as drug-like, and Kathryn Bigelow's *Strange Days* (1995) similarly viewed personal memories as a drug: both films were inspired by 1980s cyberpunk sensibilities.

As we might expect, things become even fuzzier during the next decade and a half.

2001 and Beyond

Illicit drug consumption increased from 6.3% in 2000 to 9.2% in 2012. Heroin usage was certainly a driving factor[16]; marijuana too. Though marijuana remains illegal under federal law, state ballots legalized it in 2012 in Colorado and Washington. In adolescents aged twelve-to-seventeen, there has been a concomitant decline in the perception of marijuana as harmful, which may indicate increased future usage[17]. And yet, to really get a sense of the last decade and a half, I believe we should widen the scope of our discussion and think not only about illegal drugs but, more broadly, *addiction*.

Increasingly, diverse activities seem to reflect growing obsessive/compulsive behavior among us, if not outright addiction. Illustrative of this possible macro-trend are consumption rates for prescription drugs[18], rising obesity from what some call "food addiction,"[19] unprecedented levels of television consumption[20], and a massive increase in cosmetic procedures[21]. More difficult to quantify or prove, but nonetheless frequently discussed, are sex addiction and pornography consumption rates.

Does science fiction from the last fifteen years reflect this proliferation of addictive tendencies?

The answer, as far as television shows is concerned, is a resounding yes. Drugs are now firmly embedded in science fiction shows, and their story arcs wouldn't be possible without them. A few examples: "promicin" in *The 4400* (2004-2007) is a fictional neurotransmitter that has a 50% probability of killing its user and a 50% probability of endowing them with an "ability"; the addictive "Wraith enzyme" in *Stargate: Atlantis* (2004-2008) confers humans with increased strength and speed; and "cortexiphan" in *Fringe* (2008-2013) is a nootropic, or "smart drug," that results in abilities like telekinesis, pyrokinesis, and astral projection.

Many recent films also rely heavily on drug tropes. *Equilibrium*'s (2002) "prozium" suppresses emotions, an idea that goes at least as far back as Arthur K. Barnes' short story "Emotion Solution" (1936). The first three entries in the popular *X-Men* film series (2000, 2003, 2006) deal with a mutant-inhibiting drug known simply as "the cure."

The world-wide virus unleashed in *Rise of the Planet of the Apes* (2011) is caused by the drugs "ALZ-112" and "ALZ-113." *Dredd*'s (2012) "Slo-Mo," which stretches subjective time, harkens back to the similar "tempus fugit" in Heinlein's *The Puppet Masters* (1951). And nootropics make additional appearances in the form of "NZT-48" in Neil Burger's *Limitless* (2011) and as "CPH4" in Luc Besson's *Lucy* (2014).

Regarding written science fiction, I mentioned its marked fragmentation in the 90s: if anything, this has accelerated in the years since. There are now more fantastical camps or sub-genres than ever before. As might be expected, some of these deal with drugs and addiction, while others don't.

Steampunk stories, for instance, often feature historically-appropriate drugs: in Cherie Priest's *Boneshaker* (2009), "lemon sap" is a highly addictive "yellowish, gritty, paste-like substance" distilled from a toxic mist that eventually renders its users zombie-like, while in *Tarnished* (2012), the first volume of Karina Cooper's St. Croix Chronicles, the heroine is addicted to opium and laudanum.

China Miéville's work, often associated with the New Weird, uses drugs to great effect. *Perdido Street Station* (2000), for instance, features a caterpillar that feeds on the drug "dreamshit," while *Embassytown* (2011) features addiction to a new kind of speech.

It's tempting to reassess vampire fiction, with its renewed popularity, under the lens of addiction; vampires, after all, live in a shadow world and feel an insatiable need for their next "fix" of blood. But vampire narratives tend to focus more on gender and sexual politics[22]. (There are, of course, exceptions: a notable one may be Abel Ferrara's film *The Addiction* [1995]).

Zombies, on the other hand, operate at sub-human levels, endlessly repeating a brain-damaged cycle of consumption, behavior that can better be seen as a stand-in for addiction[23].

Urban fantasy has also picked up on addiction as a theme. Jaye Wells' Prospero's War series, for instance, is founded on the notion that magic is addictive, and the author has commented that every character in the series "is affected by addiction. It's not that different from real life."[24]

Meanwhile, other specialized story forms, such as hard SF, military SF or Weird West, don't seem particularly preoccupied with the subject.

Perhaps it is science fiction writers not associated with particular subgenres who are most consistently continuing to ring interesting variations on the drug/addiction theme. In fact, we may be seeing a small renaissance of such work.

Nancy Kress' *Yesterday's Kin* (2014), though not about drugs per se, neatly literalizes the notion of drugs as changing one's personality by inventing the drug "sugarcane," which *actually* changes who one is, in the words of one of its users, into "the person he was supposed to be"—though, as it happens, that person is the never the same twice.

Maxwell Chambers, the protagonist of Henry Escaya's *The Making of Miasma* (2014), begins as an addict to "Cerulean," a drug that stimulates pattern recognition in the brain, and, through a government drug trial, is exposed to the far more dangerous and life-altering "Dobrom," triggering a massive epidemic. Daryl Gregory's *Afterparty* (2014), set in a post-smart drug revolution future, perhaps features the ultimate fictional drug: the "Numinous" provides access to divinity, or God, for each user, thereby rendering all other drugs unnecessary.

As long as science fiction continues to be concerned with questions of identity, perception, epistemology, pleasure, freedom and existentialism, it seems likely that drugs and addiction will continue to be integral parts of its narrative kit.

The genre's history shows that these are among the most versatile storytelling tools available, and can be used to zoom in or enhance any conceivable idea in all manner of recreated pasts, alternate presents, and extrapolated futures. I think it's safe to say that drugs in science fiction are here to stay.

Footnotes:

1 The novel also features the addictive mental enhancer "sapho juice."

2 Much of Philip K. Dick's work makes use of drugs, and he wrote at length on the subject (see, for example, his essay "Drugs, Hallucinations and the Quest for Reality" [1964]). Perhaps one of the most memorable fictional psychoactive drugs in his body of work is the powerful "Substance D" in *A Scanner Darkly* (1977), the book from which the title of this article is taken.

3 I invite the curious reader to seek out Robert Silverberg's *Drug Themes in Science Fiction* (1974), a critical bibliography of science fiction drug stories from 1929-1973.

4 "Soma," for example, is an instrument of distraction and repression in Aldous Huxley's *Brave New World* (1932).

5 *2014 National Drug Control Strategy - 2014 Data Supplement,* Table 2, page 24. Drug usage statistics expressed as a percentage of the population in this

article are from this source, unless otherwise noted. All drug usage and addiction references throughout this article refer to the United States.

6 See *Moral Panics: The Social Construction of Deviance* by Erich Goode & Nachman Ben-Yehuda (1994), Chapter 12, "The American Drug Panic of the 1980s."

7 For a thorough and engrossing discussion, I recommend Andrew M. Butler's book-length study *Solar Flares: Science Fiction in the 1970s* (2012), from which this term is quoted.

8 See prev.

9 It's possible, too, that with the discovery of endorphins in 1975, and various other studies regarding neurotransmitters bearing fruit, for many the notion of transcendent experience may have started to decouple from hallucinogens. Chemistry, rather than spirituality, became associated with these "trips," surely removing some of the appeal.

10 Consider Quaaludes, for example. Quaaludes (the brand name of methaqualone, first prescribed in the 1960s as a non-addictive sleeping aid) surged in popularity, particularly among teens, in the 1970s. But government initiatives had severely reduced their consumption by 1984: see page 47, "Methaqualone (1982)", of http://www.justice.gov/dea/about/history/1980-1985.pdf.

11 This last figure is based on respondents to a New York Times/CBS News poll. See *Moral Panics: The Social Construction of Deviance* by Erich Goode & Nachman Ben-Yehuda (1994), Chapter 12, "The American Drug Panic of the 1980s."

12 Figures on maximum cocaine use vary with sources. According to the Substance Abuse and Mental Health Services Administration used throughout, cocaine consumption reached an apex of 3%—5.7 million Americans—by 1985. A PBS website, on the other hand, places the maximum in 1982, and says there were 10.4 million users.

13 See *Mississippi Review*, 47/8 (1988), p. 51.

14 For an insightful discussion of Shepard's retrospective *The Best of Lucius Shepard* (2008) that comments on these stories, see Paul Kincaid's *SF Site* review at https://www.sfsite.com/08b/ls278.htm.

15 An annotated discussion may be found in "Chapter 10: The 1990s" of Roger Luckhurst's *Science Fiction* (2005).

16 Heroin usage went from 1.6% to 1.8% during this period, and resulted in more heroin-related overdoses than ever before. For a recent write-up, see http://time.com/4505/heroin-gains-popularity-as-cheap-doses-flood-the-u-s/.

17 See http://www.drugabuse.gov/news-events/nida-notes/2014/04/in-nation-wide-survey-more-students-use-marijuana-fewer-use-other-drugs.

18 In 2013, the U.S. Department of Health and Human Services issued a report titled "Addressing Prescription Drug Abuse in the United States" that contains alarming statistics, such as the fact that "opioid-related overdose deaths now outnumber overdose deaths involving all illicit drugs such as heroin and cocaine combined." Researchers at the Mayo Clinic and Olmsted Medical Center have found that "nearly 70% of Americans are on at least one prescription drug, and more than half take two."

19 More than two-thirds of U.S. adults are currently overweight or obese, and obesity rates have more than doubled in adults and children since the 1970's (see http://frac.org/initiatives/hunger-and-obesity/obesity-in-the-us/). A 2009 paper published in the *Journal of Addiction Medicine* found that "multiple but similar brain circuits are disrupted in obesity and drug addiction," and advised "that strategies aimed at improving dopamine function might be beneficial in the treatment and prevention of obesity." The American Foundation for Addiction Research has compiled a list of articles on "food addiction." Pulitzer Prize-winning reporter Michael Moss has gathered and documented a myriad ways in which the processed food industry continuously and scientifically re-engineers its product to create maximum cravings in its consumers as a means of increasing revenue in his book *Salt Sugar Fat: How the Food Giants Hooked Us* (2013).

20 In 2000 the average American man watched four hours and eleven minutes of television per day, the American woman four hours and forty-six minutes; by 2009 these figures had climbed to four hours and fifty-four minutes and five hours and thirty-one minutes respectively (see the compilation of TV-related statistics "TV Basics" assembled by the Television Bureau of Advertising). A 2012 Nielsen report found that the average American over the age of two was watching more than thirty-four hours of live television a week, in addition to three to six hours of recorded programs. An article published by Robert Kubey and Mihaly Csikszentmihalyi in *Scientific American*, "Television Addiction Is No Mere Metaphor" (February 2002), suggests a parallelism between the symptoms of drug dependency, such as withdrawal, and prolonged television consumption. According to a recent TiVo survey, the newer phenomenon of "binge watching" is increasing, too, and perceptions of it as a negative are declining among viewers. (Perhaps ironically, the most binge-watched show at the start of 2014 was *Breaking Bad* [2008-2013]).

21 According to 2013 data released by the American Society for Aesthetic Plastic Surgery, there has been a whopping 279% rise in the total number of cosmetic procedures performed in the US since 1997. During this timeframe surgical procedures (of which the five most common, in descending order, were liposuction, breast augmentation, blepharoplasty, abdominoplasty, and rhinoplasty) increased by 89%, while nonsurgical procedures increased by 521% (the five most common, in descending order, were botulinum toxin, hyaluronic acid, hair removal, microdermabrasion, and photorejuvenation). Repeat cosmetic surgery patients are also becoming more common; busi-

ness from repeat patients increased by 13% from 2009 to 2010, by 8% from 2010 to 2011, by 7% from 2011 to 2012, and again by 4% from 2012 to 2013 (see individual yearly reports at http://www.plasticsurgery.org/news/plastic-surgery-statistics.html).

22 See Jennifer Fountain's "The Vampire in Modern American Media: 1975 - 2000."

23 Zombies have often been discussed in terms of other forces, like consumerism. See, for example, Stephen Harper's "Zombies, Malls, and the Consumerism Debate: George Romero's Dawn of the Dead."

24 http://www.sfsignal.com/archives/2014/06/guest-post-special-needs-in-strange-worlds-jaye-wells-on-addiction-in-fantasy/

ABOUT THE AUTHOR

Alvaro is the co-author, with Robert Silverberg, of *When the Blue Shift Comes*, which received a starred review from *Library Journal*. Alvaro's short fiction and poetry have appeared or are forthcoming in *Analog, Nature, Galaxy's Edge, Apex* and other venues, and Alvaro was nominated for the 2013 Rhysling Award. Alvaro's reviews, critical essays and interviews have appeared in *The Los Angeles Review of Books, Strange Horizons, SF Signal, The New York Review of Science Fiction, Foundation,* and other markets. Alvaro currently edits the blog for *Locus.*

Anywhere with Pillars:
A Conversation with Jo Walton

ALVARO ZINOS-AMARO

Jo Walton has published ten novels, three poetry collections and an essay collection, with another two novels due out in 2015. She won the John W. Campbell Award for Best New Writer in 2002, the World Fantasy Award in 2004 for *Tooth and Claw,* and the Hugo and Nebula awards in 2012 for *Among Others.* She comes from Wales but lives in Montreal where the food and books are much better. She writes science fiction and fantasy, reads a lot, talks about books, and eats great food. She plans to live to be ninety-nine and write a book every year.

I first learned of Jo Walton's work when I heard about *Tooth and Claw.* Dragons by way of Anthony Trollope? I was hooked. After that I regularly sought out her fiction, and Jo's fiery *Tor.com* posts quickly became an addiction. It was therefore a real treat, though a bit unnerving, to moderate her on a panel about the Retro Hugos at the most recent Worldcon. I shouldn't have worried. The panel went well—all I had to do was get out of the way of Jo and the other participants. In fact, it went well enough for Jo to take time out of her busy schedule a few months later to answer some questions for me . . .

I love your character names. What's your process for coming up with them, and how early or late does it happen in your overall creative process?

Many of my characters arrive with names. Others don't. Early in the process of a project I'll make an alphabetized list of culture-appropriate names, and grab one when I need it. Often I'll know already where in the alphabet I want the name to come, and sometimes the kind of sounds I want, because I'll have an idea of the character's personality. If I don't, if it's a case of somebody coming through the door with a gun and I snatch a name at random, they'll get a lot of their personality from being called Wendy, with its wide open beginning and snapped shut end, and its roots in J.M. Barrie.

The question of how somebody whose parents named them after the motherly little girl who *did* want to grow up got to the point of picking up that gun and be coming through the door with it will be part of the character's history. This will (naturally) be completely invisible to the reader in most cases, but it's very useful to me when it comes to how a character will talk and behave.

Names always come very early in the process. If I have to change a character name it's a huge painful thing, and it changes the character. I think about names a lot. Names are charged and powerful and pull in different directions. They have historical and mythological resonance, they have sound resonance, and they have class resonance—whether the reader recognizes that or not. They also have dates, when you're working in this world. Someone named Ashley is a certain age and class, for instance. In a different world, then the reader won't already know what a name denotes, but it will still have that kind of context, and I'll be thinking about that. You can use names to do worldbuilding and convey context—people from different societies will have different kinds of names.

After reading your posts for Tor.com, I'm curious if you maintain a reading log that tracks your reading activity, including the titles of the books you've read and when you've finished them (and how many times you've read them!).

No, I don't. I read for pleasure, keeping databases would be boring. I do have a Goodreads account and I do update it sometimes. I certainly don't track how many times I've read something, whatever for?

There's a competitive element to the way some people talk about reading—x many books, x many times read—that is really strange to me. I've been accused of boasting about how fast I read when I mention it on *Tor.com,* so I've stopped talking about it. I really do read entirely for fun.

What are the two or three books you think you've re-read most often in your life? How many times roughly have you re-read them, and do you expect to continue returning to these titles with the same fervor in the future?

The problem is not that they lose their appeal, the problem is that I learn them by heart, so I can't read them any more, because I can recite them. I can't sink into them and be caught up because I know all the words.

Things I've read the most times—*The Lord of the Rings.* Cherryh's Union/Alliance books. Bujold's Miles books. *The Dispossessed. Stars in My Pockets Like Grains of Sand.* Rosemary Kirstein's Steerswoman books. Mary Renault.

I don't let myself read things more than once a year, so theoretically I haven't read anything more than fifty times, but I didn't institute that rule until I started having problems with how often I was reading *Cyteen* so I don't know.

Each of your books or trilogies seems to tackle new forms or sub-genres, keeping readers delightfully on their toes. In several posts you've mentioned your enjoyment of military SF, by authors such as Jerry Pournelle or David Weber. Is military SF something you might consider for a future project?

You never know. But I find SF much more difficult than fantasy, because for fantasy you have history to lean on, and for SF you have to make it all up.

Setting really informs your fiction: you evoke a strong sense of place in all of your stories. I imagine you're good at researching places, or well traveled, or most likely a combination of both. What are some of the places you've most enjoyed visiting—"anywhere with pillars," as one character teases in your forthcoming The Just City (2015)?

I'm not all that well traveled. My friend the thriller writer Jon Evans has been everywhere. I've been to quite a lot of places in Europe, and generally when I travel in North America I go by train, which means I see a lot more places and landscapes than people who fly.

Place is very important to me, and in fact all the places in all my books are real and I have been to them. I need to feel a sense of connection to a place to write about it. But that can happen quite fast. In 2011 I spent a week in Florence staying with my friend Ada Palmer (whose brilliant *Dogs of Peace* is coming out from Tor next year) and I just fell in love with it, and it has been appearing in everything I've written since, including things set in Heaven, on generation starships, and in Plato's Republic. I have been back there every year since.

What are a few destinations you've never traveled to but you would like to visit in the future?

Of course, I'd like to go everywhere . . . I want to go to Naples, and Istanbul, and lots of places in Asia, and to other planets, and of course Ithaca, but only the Ship of Fools is traveling there this year . . .

In your novel, Among Others, to what degree were the authors and books a conscious choice on your part, designed to help illuminate the character of Mori to the reader, and to what degree were they instinctively autobiographical, drawn directly from your own memories of reading?

Lots of both. My memories of reading and my reactions to books when I was that age really guided me a lot—and her likes and dislikes are very congruent with mine when I was that age. But what she reads when and her response to it was definitely chosen deliberately—for instance *Babel 17* being the book she is halfway through at the time when she chooses not to die, when *Babel 17* is about communication and connection.

I'm curious if you also read what we might think of as "associational" SF books—that is, books written by SF authors that are not SF. I'm thinking particularly of nonfiction, but also non-genre novels by primarily genre authors. If so, do you have any favorites?

Yes, of course I do. Dan Simmons *Phases of Gravity*, Susan Palwick's *Mending the Moon*, John Brunner's *The Great Steamboat Race*, Keith

Roberts's *The Boat of Fate*, L. Sprague de Camp's *An Elephant for Aristotle*, everything Marge Piercy and Margaret Atwood and Kazuo Ishiguro and Doris Lessing and Anthony Burgess wrote that wasn't SF . . . no, wait, that wasn't what you're asking!

As for nonfiction, I guess I have read Le Guin and Delany and Tolkien's essays, but I can't think of much else. Most of the non fiction I read is history and biography and things.

Given your fascination with classical philosophy and mythology, I'm curious if you've read other SF writer's takes on some of these raw materials—Dan Simmons' Ilium and Olympos, to quote a recent example, or others?

I haven't read those. I can't think of much actually. Lots of historical fiction that's on the edge of fantasy—Mary Renault especially.

Any others besides Renault?

More classical historical fiction on the edge of fantasy—Gillian Bradshaw, Georgia Sallska's *Priam's Daughter*, Alfred Duggan.

In one your posts on Tor.com you classified book series according to four broad categories (I'm using my own words here):

1. *single books split up into multiple volumes on publication*

2. *series where each book is self-contained but reading them in the correct order is recommended*

3. *series that can be read in any order, but which benefit from cumulative reading*

4. *series made of up self-contained volumes that are completely independent of each other.*

I noticed that your website refers to your next novel, The Just City, as the first of the new three-book Thessaly series. Which of the above categories best describes this forthcoming series (or did you invent a fifth one)? And at what point in the development of the ideas/characters did you realize it would be three volumes?

It's a type 2 series, definitely.

Each book is self-contained, and I could have stopped at the end of book one, or at the end of book two. When I'd finished *The Just City*, I knew I'd have to either write an extra chapter covering some things left dangling, or write a sequel. I thought about it, and wrote *The Philosopher Kings*. Then when I'd finished that, it could have been enough, but then I looked through a solar telescope in the Lowell Observatory in Flagstaff and knew I had to write the third one.

So are you currently working on the third volume, Necessity?

Yes, I am working on *Necessity*, or I would be if I wasn't doing this interview.

ABOUT THE AUTHOR

Alvaro is the co-author, with Robert Silverberg, of *When the Blue Shift Comes*, which received a starred review from *Library Journal*. Alvaro's short fiction and poetry have appeared or are forthcoming in *Analog, Nature, Galaxy's Edge, Apex* and other venues, and Alvaro was nominated for the 2013 Rhysling Award. Alvaro's reviews, critical essays and interviews have appeared in *The Los Angeles Review of Books, Strange Horizons, SF Signal, The New York Review of Science Fiction, Foundation,* and other markets. Alvaro currently edits the blog for *Locus*.

Another Word:
Free Advice from a Full-Time Author.
Worth Every Penny Paid
WESLEY CHU

I'm going to start by admitting that I don't know what I'm talking about. Nevertheless, I am a full-time writer and my path to achieving my lifelong dream isn't some quest where the rickety bridge collapsed behind me right after I crossed it. I didn't grab the only McGuffin along the way as I laid waste to the publishing gatekeepers. In other words, you can probably follow in my footsteps if you desire. Do you actually want to? You may not by the time this article is through, but, if you do, that's your prerogative. *Don't say you weren't warned.*

Full-time writing is a lot like parenthood, without having to change diapers as often. Mind you, I have no children. Since we've already established that I don't really know I'm talking about, let's assume you trust me when I say you have to deal with a lot of shit. In the early days, writing will keep spitting up on your shirt and everyone will think what you're doing is "cute."

It's easy to get discouraged. It's easy to feel like you're wasting your damn time doing this stringing-words-together thing hoping to achieve some unattainable goal that seemingly requires pulling blackjack every hand for an hour. Well, you're not.

You, my writing padawan, are acquiring necessary skills. You're assembling a writing toolbox. You're learning to fail. And fail you will, a crap ton of times as you learn that this metaphorical Phillips screwdriver doesn't work for squat trying to metaphorically caulk this metaphorical hole in the wall. I know, I know. It's all fun and metaphors until someone gets cut.

Let's go back to the parenthood analogy. You're nurturing this writing baby and your desperate hope is that this baby grows up to be a productive member of society and not a serial killer or say, the screenwriter for the *Transformers* movie. (Yes I know he's rich.) Let's be honest, does that dude look in the mirror every morning and say, "You, sir, are one hell of a writer?" Okay, he probably does. But, when he dies, and stands at the Pearly Gates, and the gatekeeper (always these gatekeepers!) looks at his resume and sees *Age of Extinction,* I think we all know where he's going. Eternal paradise isn't in his cards.

Regardless, honing these necessary skills will take time before you "go pro" (and by that I mean someone out there decides that something you've written is worth real tangible money). It could be ten years from the first time you sat down to write. It could be the next day (I hate you). Whatever amount of time it takes is the time it takes. I won't judge you and you shouldn't judge yourself.

Let's say you're there already. You've assembled that writing toolbox. You've nurtured your writing career like the mewling babe it is and you "think" you're ready to write full time. The path to full-time writing is usually slow unless you're incredibly lucky (I hate you) or a supremely talented individual (I hate you more) that somehow made it big on your first time up to bat (more confusing metaphors!). Thusly, I'm willing to bet you probably work a day job or live with your parents. This is the time in your writing career where you do what you have to survive: serving coffee, programming, veterinarian-ing. This could last for a few years or the rest of your life. I'll write an article someday about holding down a full-time job and writing part time. I'll call it *Time Management and Self-Immolation.*

How will you know when it's time to make the leap and become a full-time writer? Well, you won't know when until you know you have to. How's that for advice? The common wisdom I've received from almost every career writer is that you work that day job until you can't. You work that day job until you're just juggling too much and something has to give. In my case, I got laid off and said screw it, I'm going for it. Technically, I kept to the exact wording of "work that day job until I can't" though I'm pretty sure I violated the spirit of that statement. Goes to show how much my wisdom is worth, eh?

Let's assume you have a day job, and you have a semblance of a writing career that's starting to take off. Suddenly, you're at Robert Frost's two roads diverging in the yellow wood. You need to figure out which path to take. Do you keep your soul-sucking functional tolerable wonderful job and write part time? Or do you say screw it (metaphorical screwdriver and all), I'm going for it? There's no wrong answer to this. You do what you feel is right. However, here are a few questions to keep in mind:

Do you like your day job more than writing? If the answer is yes, don't quit. Wow. This is easy.

Are you a huge fan of financial security and retirement? If the answer is yes, don't quit. I personally plan to write until I die. Really, this advice thing isn't so hard. Eat your heart out, Wendig.

Do you like stability? If the answer is yes, don't quit. This might be getting repetitive.

Do you like only working forty hours a week? If yes, and assuming your current day job is a straight nine to fiver, then don't quit. Full-time writing is an all-encompassing seven-days/sixty-hours-a-week job with awful job security—and when I say awful, I mean none—and even worse medical. We sit on our asses a lot which is terrible for our health. That's another future article: *Sitting on Our Asses Is Terrible for Our Health.*

Lastly, is money more important to you than a writing career? If the answer is yes, then don't quit.*

Wait: let me put an asterisk on that last question. There. You probably read the asterisk before you read this sentence. It's kind of like a time travel thing just now, isn't it? Oh yeah, my time travel book, *Time Salvager,* is coming out in July 2015. How's that for name dropping? That will be another future article: *Marketing Yourself: The Funny, the Subtle, and You.*

Anyway, the asterisk is because there are many variables to consider when comparing writing income to day-job income.

For example, what's your dang day job?

If you're a doctor, you'll probably make more with your day job.

If you're a garbage man, you'll probably make more with your day job.

If you're flipping burgers at McDonalds, you'll probably make more with your day job.

This is why at conventions people call me Wesley the Optimist.

Admittedly, there are many successful writers who make a pretty respectable living, and a couple who make it huge. Major props to those folks, but writing, as a career, is a feast or famine field. Ninety-five percent of us eke out a living, while the select few sit on their pile of treasure like Smaug. Do I have exact metrics? No, but I'm willing to wager my last dollar bill that it's probably true. (Please don't take that dollar from me.)

There is something to be said about the currency of doing what you love. If you love writing, and I don't know any career writers who don't, then that currency has a value to you that, added with the actual currency you earn as a writer, minus your financial obligations to adulthood, can help you decide whether making that full-time writing decision is the right one for you.

So there you have it.

I just want to remind you that I stated at the very beginning of this article that I have no idea what I'm talking about. Take everything I wrote with a grain of salt. It's not an easy path to take, and definitely one less traveled. It's extraordinarily rewarding with massive highs and some kick-you-in-the-gut lows. As someone who's worked in the corporate black hole for almost twenty years, I can safely say that this is the most difficult thing I've ever done and it is the hardest I've ever worked for the least amount of money but I would make this choice all over again.

My final piece of advice? There will be many things you'll have to do when you cross that full-time bridge other than telling stories.

For example, I am getting paid by the word for this article.

Editor's note: No he isn't. We clearly communicated through a barrage of flaming arrows and carrier pigeons that the Another Word pieces are paid a flat rate (no matter how many words are crammed onto the page). We invite you to come back at an undetermined time to view Wesley's upcoming piece on reading the fine print titled, "How to Avoid Flaming Bird Shit—a.k.a, Dealing with Editors."

Author's Note: Last piece of advice. Read your contracts and rates before writing articles!

ABOUT THE AUTHOR

Wesley Chu's best friend is Michael Jordan, assuming that best friend status is earned by a shared television commercial. If not, then his best friend is his dog Eva who he can often be seen riding like a trusty steed through the windy streets of Chicago.

In 2014, Wesley Chu was shortlisted for the John W. Campbell Best New Writer Award. Chu's debut novel, *The Lives of Tao,* earned him a Young Adult Library Services Association Alex Award and a Science Fiction Goodreads Choice Award Finalist slot. The sequel, *The Deaths of Tao,* continues the story of secret agent Roen Tan and his sarcastic telepathically bonded alien, Tao.

Chu has two books scheduled for 2015. The last book in the Tao trilogy, *The Rebirths of Tao,* is coming out April 7th. *Time Salvager,* published by Tor Books, featuring an energy stealing time traveler with addiction issues, is slated for July 7th, 2015.

Editor's Desk:
Translation Is Important
NEIL CLARKE

Telepathy, universal translators, and other convenient tricks allow our favorite science fiction characters to bypass the inherent problems in communicating across multiple languages. It's a simple shortcut and recognizable trope that allows the author to keep the story moving. We often have trouble with the language barriers among our fellow humans, so it's not hard to imagine how much could go wrong between species.

The way we address language and communication in science fiction has been bouncing around in my head a lot lately. Wouldn't it be nice to have a magical device to solve this problem? Sure, we have things like Google Translate and they can be quite helpful, but it's still communication on a very childlike level. Machine translation doesn't understand the context or cultural references. That might be acceptable for bookshelf assembly instructions, but it would completely strip a story of its strengths.

Stories require someone who is intimately familiar with the language, culture, and storytelling. I've often said that I think a good translator has to empathize with the writer they are translating or the story could suffer. These complications—and the addition expense of translation—have left most English-speaking markets isolated from science fiction happening in other languages.

I've always felt like we were missing out on something.

In the last few years, I've had the privilege to work with two excellent writers who also happen to be translators: Ken Liu and John Chu. It's thanks to their efforts that we've been able to publish several Chinese translations over the last few years. Those rewarding experiences led to our partnership with Storycom and last month's successful Kickstarter campaign to regularly publish stories from other languages.

This January, we'll publish the first of many Chinese translations—every other month for the first six months and every month after that—as a supplement to our regular content!

I'm absolutely overjoyed by the warm reception our plans received from readers and other parts of our community. While the focus of this project was Chinese science fiction, we never intended to stop there. Thanks to some generous support, it won't. I am very pleased to say that we've been able to establish a small translation fund to help us secure stories from even more languages. We don't have a solid timetable for those stories, but during the last month, we've heard from many translators and fans from around the world. From that base, we'll build the infrastructure we need to get that project running.

Along those lines, a reader asked me why we decided to go with a regular feature over a special issue or anthology. It's a good question, particularly in light of how fashionable the latter has become in recent years. While I don't think there is anything wrong with special issues, I'm not a big fan of the one-and-done model of promoting a cause. They might make a big splash and generate some warm fuzzies, but months later, it's largely forgotten.

I want translations to become something normal. They shouldn't stand out or be special because of where they originate. Regularly publishing stories from other parts of the world is the best way to do that. If something is important, make it part of who you are.

This *is* important. It will be part of who we are. No gimmicks. Just stories.

ABOUT THE AUTHOR

Neil Clarke is the editor of *Clarkesworld Magazine,* owner of Wyrm Publishing and three-time Hugo Award Nominee for Best Editor (short form). He currently lives in NJ with his wife and two children.

About the Artist

SANDEEP KARUNAKARAN

Kuldar Leement is a twenty-seven-year-old concept artist. He studied technical drawing and general building for three years at the Kehtna Economy and Technology School. He then studied graphic design at the Tartu Art School before becoming employed by Tabasco Ad Agency, where he is an illustrator.

WEBSITE

www.kuldarleement.eu/id

www.ingramcontent.com/pod-product-compliance
Lightning Source LLC
Chambersburg PA
CBHW020309150626
46552CB00022B/2547